Brother Petroc's Return

S.M.C.

2012
DNS Publication

Brother Petroc's Return by S.M.C. was originally published in 1937 by Little, Brown and Company. This 2012 edition by DNS Publications contains the original text with the addition of translations of the Latin passages.

Copyright © 1964 English Dominican Sisters
of Saint Catherine of Siena

All rights reserved. No part of this book may be reproduced, stored in a retrieval system, or transmitted in any form, or by any means, electronic, mechanical, photocopying, or otherwise, without the prior written permission of the publisher or the congregation of the English Dominican Sisters of Saint Catherine of Siena, except by a reviewer, who may quote brief passages in a review.

Printed in the United States of America

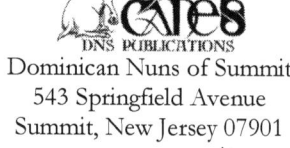

Dominican Nuns of Summit
543 Springfield Avenue
Summit, New Jersey 07901
www.nunsopsummit.org

ISBN: 1478269987
ISBN-13: 978-1478269984

It would be both ungracious and ungrateful to describe my familiar friends, Brother Petroc, the Abbot and the Subprior as fiction; so I will content myself with saying that my tale is founded on a Hypothesis, which is not at all impossible in the universe to which it belongs. Granted this Hypothesis, the rest is inevitable; even to the purchase of S. Brioc by the English Benedictines. This explanation will, I think, be sufficient for those to whom it is due.

-S.M.C.

Books by the Same Author

A Treasure of Joy and Gladness

And No Birds Sing

Angel of the Judgment

As the Clock Struck Twenty

Brother Petroc's Return

Children Under Fire

The Chronicles of Thomas Frith, O.P.

The Dark Wheel

The Flight and the Song

Henry Suso: A Saint and Poet

Jacek of Poland

Margaret, Princess of Hungary

Once in Cornwall

The Spark in the Reeds

Steward of Souls

Storm out of Cornwall

Chapter One

Brother Petroc lay dying; that is, if he were not already dead.

Outside the Monastery, scarcely a hundred yards from the edge of the cliff, the surf of the ever-restless Atlantic beat on the wild north Cornish shore, and a fine mist of spray blew in, as it always did, at the narrow unglazed window of the cell. But the crash of breakers and the screaming of gulls had no power to disturb Brother Petroc, who lay with closed eyes on his pallet, serene and motionless; so still that even the gradually weakening breathing seemed to have stopped at last.

Presently there was a sound of steps along the corridor outside; the doors opened and my Lord Abbot, followed by the Infirmarian, entered the cell. He was a tall, dignified figure of a man, scarcely past his prime; but his forehead was knit with many wrinkles, and the hair that had escaped the tonsure was snow-white; for my Lord Abbot lived in difficult times and had seen more than a little trouble. He crossed the room and stood by the bed-side, looking down on the still form, with pursed lips and narrow, scrutinizing eyes. After a moment's survey he bent down and placed his hand first on the pulse, then on the heart. He made a little sign to the Brother and sank on his knees:

"*De profundis clamavi ad te, Domine,*" said my Lord Abbot, and there was an unmistakable note of relief in his voice. The Brother Infirmarian kneeling beside him took up the alternate verses.

The Psalm ended, the Abbot rose, turned quickly from the dead man and spoke in sharp decisive tones:

"Tell the Prior to ring the bell and summon the Brethren," he said. "Let the Sacristan have the stone ready to close the vault, and mortar to fasten it. The Lay Brothers must provision the boats and get them ready to launch; tell the Procurator to see to that. Find two young monks and bring them here. Between you, you must carry Brother Petroc, as he is, down to the Choir. We must bury him immediately, and then row out as quickly as possible to Long Island. I have decided that our only chance of safety will be to live in the caves there until this storm blows over. Then, by God's Grace, in a few weeks we shall return and finish Brother Petroc's funeral rites in a more seemly fashion. Also"—he added as the Infirmarian turned to go—"find the Cantor and tell him to prepare a paper giving the deceased Brother's name and date of Profession, stating also that he died on the eve of his ordination day.

I must see to the hiding of what few valuables we have."

The Abbot turned and hurried out of the cell, followed by the Infirmarian. He was not really cold or heartless; but he had endured trouble enough to try even the most patient man, and Brother Petroc's sudden illness and death had happened most inopportunely. For this was August 14th in the year of grace 1549.

Two days before this, my Lord Abbot was sitting in the great chair in his room in the North Cloister. The door was open and from where he sat he could see the Brethren at work in their carrals. A circular illuminated calendar with an elaborate plan of the heavenly houses gave the date August 12th, and the year of our Lord 1549. On the broad window-ledge, hastily staying themselves with large pasties and small beer, sat three scarecrows of men, and as they munched the Abbot plied them with questions.

"We were doing right well, my Lord," they told him between bites; "we had taken

Launceston and had well repaid the traitor Greville for the death of Kylter and the rest last year. Then at S. Mary's Clyst we were worsted by the heretic army. The S. Brioc men were on the left wing and somehow we were cut off from the rest. We were sore beset by a band thrice our size and after fierce fighting the few of us who were left fled for home. The heretics are close behind us, so we turned off here on our way to the village to tell you and the Brethren to hasten to the caves in Long Island and wait there in hiding until the storm blows over."

"We are much indebted to you and the rest, Tregantle, for remembering us in your own distress. I will take measures as soon as may be for the safety of my monks."

The Abbot rose and, signing to the Guest Master standing outside to take charge of the men, hurried to the Procurator's room to begin preparations. After all he was not quite unprepared. For life had been difficult and living precarious for several years now.

That the Benedictine Abbey of S. Brioc was still in the possession of its lawful owners was because it was a very small poor place, perched on a high bleak headland of the north Cornish coast. It was an unpretentious building of rough granite blocks, unenclosed save for the quadrangle shut in by its own cloisters. It was right off the track of any of the great roads, with no town nearer than Polgarth five miles away.

The Monastery was built on the height of a great cliff, but to east and west the land dipped suddenly into two narrow and warmly sheltered valleys, watered by tiny swift streams and leading down to a patch of shingle. Such valleys as these are found all along that coast. The valley to the west belonged to the monks, who kept a few cows and sheep and contrived to till sufficient land to yield a scant livelihood of corn and vegetables. That to the east held a large village peopled by wild, silent folk, who quarried the slate which was plentiful in that district, and fished, turning wreckers in a body when occasion served. They obeyed the monks only when it suited them, but loved them with an almost dog-like devotion.

His Majesty's Commissioners had never even heard of the Abbey, for the Bishop of Exeter had diplomatically forgotten its existence when he filled in the list of Religious Houses for his diocese; it was neither rich nor large enough to tempt an informer; beside which, the people round about were all Catholics, and a Cornishman never betrays his fellows to up-country foreigners. So the monks lived in peace and served the village as though England still owned allegiance to Rome. There was only one significant change made, when a special Rescript came from Rome consecrating the Abbot a bishop, with power to ordain his own monks.

But after a time there filtered through to this wild solitary spot—as all such news does filter through—a tale of Humphrey Arundell gathering a band of Cornish men to march into Devon and put to flight those King's men who were striving to introduce by force an English Version of prayers, instead of their own Latin Mass Book; and that too when half the men of Cornwall were far more ignorant of the English than the Latin tongue. So the men of S. Brioc's had unearthed all that might serve as weapons of offence and defense, and hastened to join the band, ten thousand strong, who were marching east.

At first their prospects had been good and their hopes high; but at S. Mary's Clyst they had met with their first reverse, where the S. Brioc's contingent had been decimated and had fallen back in the direction of their own district, followed by a band detached for the purpose. This defeat had been followed by two more, which had destroyed a great part of the Catholic army, the remnant falling back in disorder on Launceston, hotly pursued by the King's men who were determined once and for all to break the spirit of the Cornish and stamp out their religion.

The Procurator's room was on the south side of the House, and the Abbot was passing the

Church door when he heard a thud and suppressed cry from the Lady Chapel beyond. He opened the door and looked in. There, stretched apparently lifeless on the floor, lay the deacon Petroc. Poor fellow! Another postponement to his ordination would be one result of the afternoon's news, and he had already waited some years beyond time.

As the Abbot hurried towards the prostrate figure the Sacristan, also roused by the noise, hastened from another direction, and both joined in raising him. Except for a faint flutter of breath there was no sign of life.

"We had better carry him upstairs to the Infirmary," said the Abbot. "The Infirmarian must do what he can to restore him as quickly as possible, for we shall have to leave the Monastery as soon as may be."

So between them they carried Petroc to the cell upstairs, and the Sacristan went in search of the Infirmarian.

"Do what you can to restore Brother Petroc," the Superior told the latter. "This is probably the effect of bad news. A messenger came from his father this afternoon to tell him that both his brothers had been slain outside Launceston. Poor lad! It has been a sad shock."

The Abbot swung quickly out of the room and went in search of the Procurator. The first necessity was to arrange for a speedy evacuation of the Abbey, taking sufficient provisions to tie the community over for some time.

So for two days the Abbot had waited, in growing perturbation, for the sick man to rally or die. Now, on the afternoon of the second day, death seemed to have intervened. There was nothing for it therefore but to bury Petroc in all haste and to escape, for the soldiers were reported to be only twelve miles distant.

The Infirmarian clothed Petroc in his habit, and carried the body down to the Choir. The Abbot sprinkled the corpse with holy water and said the Prayer customary when a body is brought to the Church. Then they lifted it into the niche in the wall, folded the hands over a Crucifix, and slipped under them the paper prepared by the Cantor. The Sacristan and his assistant fixed in the slab and made all safe. Then they left Petroc to his rest.

On the conclusion of this short ceremony the monks left the Church as quickly as possible and hurried to the strand. The boats were launched and they rowed to Long Island, a mile out to sea. There they made themselves as comfortable as they could in the caves and waited for the storm to pass.

Meanwhile the soldiery descended on the village and put all they could find to the sword, while the more prudent hid down the coast. For six weeks the King's men infested the neighborhood, but it was a matter of three months before the survivors dared return to their homes. As soon as a sufficient number had collected, they decided to row out to Long Island and see how the monks had fared. So they patched up one of their boats, and made the best of their way thither with the outgoing tide.

As they neared the island they were much distressed to find fragments of planks and spars floating on the waves, for they knew by this token that the monks' boats must have been destroyed in one of the heavy storms that rise without warning on that coast.

As they rowed up to the small beach on the landward side, they shouted and called, but only the echoes answered. They landed, beached the boat and hastened round to the caves on the northern shore. In one they found a Crucifix placed on a small flat stone slab, while in a corner there were three or four books neatly piled. In another cave they found the charred remains of a fire and other scattered signs of occupation. They climbed to the cliff above and there they found more traces of the monks; for two low mounds, each surmounted by a rude cross made of two pieces of driftwood, gave sad indication of sickness and trouble. Nowhere on the island could they find any other sign either of the late occupants, or of their fate; so the search party was driven to conclude that impelled by hunger the survivors had attempted to reach the mainland but that, weakened by sickness and lack of food, they had been unable in some sudden squall to guide the boats, which had therefore capsized.

In dejected silence the rescue party made the best of their way back to the mainland. They were now without priests or Sacraments; what wonder is it, therefore, that there was a gradual decay of faith until, two generations later, there was not a Catholic left in S. Brioc? The Monastery was not worth the consideration of those who enriched themselves by Church lands, so it was left to fall into ruin on its wild cliff.

Alone therefore of all his Brethren, within sound of the ever-fretting Atlantic, Brother Petroc slept in his old home in peace.

Chapter Two

There was a good deal of surprise and discussion in S. Brioc, the little town in the valley, when it was known that the Monastery from which it had taken its name was for sale.

How the half-ruined place had come into the hands of the Pendarwith family matters little to this tale. The fact remains that, impoverished by war taxation and heart-broken at the loss of his only son and heir, William Pendarwith decided to sell this and other estates which were not entailed, in order to secure the future of his two daughters. There was still greater surprise, and no little dismay, when it was known that the purchasers were Catholics and, worse still, monks. The explanation however was simple enough; Catholic churches on the north coast of Cornwall were few and far between and the diocese was short of priests; so when the place had been put up for sale, on very favorable terms, the Bishop had approached the English Benedictines with a request that they would buy this pre-Reformation Benedictine Abbey in order that the Abbey Church might serve the rapidly growing town of S. Brioc and the surrounding district.

For the fishing village of 1549 had grown into a small but thriving town, half seaport, half summer-resort. Added to this, artists had begun to find the surrounding scenery unrivalled of its kind, and had settled in various bungalows on the outskirts.

The English Benedictines had been generous in their response to the Bishop's appeal. The existing building was found to be easily adaptable to modern needs; and by the year 1929 the Abbey had been already occupied for some years, while the Community found itself in a position to enlarge the existing Church. An extension was to be made to that part of the building which was used by the public, and in order to do this it was necessary to utilize the existing Lady Chapel and to build a new one, which would entail the making of an entrance through the wall just below the monks' choir, and the disturbance of two or three old graves. Other vaults had been made and it was decided to translate the remains with some ceremony, before the masons should begin work.

One evening in April therefore, just as the setting sun was making mosaics on the Choir floor, the monks came in procession, headed by Cross and Acolytes, to rebury all that time had spared of their pre-Reformation brethren. They reached the first vault, which strangely enough had no inscription of any kind on its enclosing slab; then they separated, forming two lines, through which the Abbot, accompanied by Prior and Subprior, might pass. Two lay brothers with the necessary implements were already waiting by the vault.

The three Superiors made an interesting study as they stood before the grave. The Abbot was an old man, tall, thin and ascetic-looking. His eyes were the most striking thing about him, dark and piercing, but full nevertheless of an expression of so much benignity that one instinctively recognized the Father. He had entered the Monastery very young, and his knowledge of and undoubted gift in dealing with souls resulted rather from contemplation than from direct experience; for where can a man learn more safely the science of directing others than by seeing souls mirrored, as it were, in God?

The Prior was of a very different stamp. A secular priest, ordained shortly before 1914, he acted as Military Chaplain right through the war, and had then asked for admission to the Benedictine Novitiate. He was an excellent and most conscientious man, who would willingly have died in the performance of his duty as he saw it. His vision however was not a very wide one.

In many ways the Subprior was the most interesting individual of the three. The eldest son of Catholic parents, he had decided while still a boy that he wanted to be a doctor. After a most successful studentship at Guy's he had obtained brilliant results at his examinations. Then, when the prospects of his life were brightest and a great career seemed open before him, he suddenly threw it all up to become a Benedictine. The step had been a costly one, which had left its mark in the stern lines of his mouth and chin. His was a fine face, but it still lacked something which effort and suffering had been unable to give. The duties of Subprior in a Benedictine Monastery not being very arduous, he had likewise been appointed Infirmarian; an office which in that house was also something of a sinecure, since the majority of the monks were young and strong and a very capable lay brother did most of the actual nursing which was necessary.

When the Superiors reached the head of the files, the Cantor intoned the *De Profundis* which was chanted by each choir alternately; the Abbot sang the Prayer, then he signed to the two lay brothers to remove the slab. Very carefully they loosened the mortar which held it in place and then still more carefully lifted out the stone.

There was one swift, indrawn breath of surprise as the assembled monks saw the slab lowered; for within the niche was an incorrupt body. It was that of a young monk lying with hands folded round a wooden Crucifix. He was dressed in his habit, though strangely enough he had no cowl. The black cloth was worn threadbare and seemed ready to fall into dust as the air stirred it. The young man's hair and beard were long and black, the skin was olive but appeared almost to glow with a tint of life. Under the folded hands, beneath the Crucifix, there rested a sheet of parchment. The Abbot read:

"*Hic iacet Frater Petroc Trelant, Monachus. Qui ante diem undevigesimum Kalendas Septembris, anno*

Domini milesimo quingentesimo quadragesimo nono obdormivit in oculo Domini, anno aetatis sui vigesimo septimo, professionis octavo. Requiescat in pace. Si vixerat, cras ordinates fuerit. Quam celerrime eum sepelimus, quod milites impiisimi Regis appropinquant."[*]

With great reverence and no little awe the Abbot gazed on the young face; but his astonishment was redoubled when he saw the eyelids move. Very slowly they were raised and a pair of brown eyes looked at him with an expression of blank languor. The monks, who had involuntarily moved forward and now stood in a semicircle round the vault, were petrified, watching while the lids dropped again. A second time they were raised, this time for a fraction of

---

[*] "Here lies Brother Petroc Trelant, Monk, who slept in the presence of the Lord on the 21st day before the Kalends of September,[*] in the Year of Our Lord 1549, in the 27th year of his age, the 8th of his profession. May he rest in peace. Had he lived, he would have been ordained tomorrow. We are burying him in the greatest haste, since the soldiers of the most impious King are drawing near."

[*August 14th]

time longer, then a second time they drooped over the brown eyes, while a faint but unmistakable sigh was heard. There was a gasp, and a movement as if for flight, from the now terrified Community. But the Subprior, gathering his self-control, stepped up and laid a finger on the wrist.

"I can feel some sort of a pulse here," he said; "it is incredible, but I really believe the man is alive. If you will have the Choir cleared I will see what I can do for him"; and he hurried out of the Church.

The Abbot turned and in a whisper bade his Community disperse.

"But remember," he added, "there is to be no discussion of the matter even among yourselves, until I can leave the place and speak to you in the Chapter House."

As the monks slipped quietly away, they met the Subprior returning with a tray on which there were brandy and other things which he thought might be of service. By the time he reached the vault, there was no one left but the Abbot and the Lay Brother who acted as his assistant.

Together they worked for the matter of an hour, a time of sharp anxiety and varying hope. Life hung on a very slight thread. Sometimes the pulse would stop altogether and after a second or two recommence its feeble beat. The breathing alternately strengthened and ceased; it seemed as if the fresh air brought renewed life, while its very vitalizing power almost extinguished the feeble flame it had fanned. They dared not move the lad—for in spite of his seven and twenty years, he looked little more—from the niche where he lay, lest the handling necessary to do so should prove fatal. So they tended him as best they could there in his tomb.

At length the pulse began to steady and strengthen while the breathing grew regular and a faint tinge of color appeared in cheeks and lips. After watching the young man attentively, with his hand on the pulse, the Subprior at last ventured to trickle a few drops of brandy between the parted lips. He watched the effect anxiously, and there was a movement of relief from the three as they saw a distinct motion of swallowing in the throat muscles. The Subprior waited a few minutes, then cautiously administered a second dose. Then the eyes opened and the head turned.

The Abbot bent over him. "Brother," he said, very gently but distinctly, "do not be afraid. You are safe, with your own Brethren."

There was no response in the eyes, but from the lips came a faint murmur. The Subprior also bent down to catch the words, and then with a sudden shock realized that Elizabethan English, pronounced by a Cornishman, so differed in tone, modulation and accent from modern speech, that they and this new-found Brother of theirs could not understand each other. Their own language was no means of communication between them, and it was obvious that unless some way of conveying a notion of safety and friendship were found the situation would rapidly become desperate, for with returning intelligence bewilderment was fast giving place to terror and the Subprior foresaw grave danger to the poor, half-stunned mind.

Before matters reached a crisis however the Abbot found a solution to the difficulty. Very slowly he spoke, bending close to the sick man:

"*Noli timere, amici sumus, Deus tibi curavit.*"[*]

Three times he repeated these few words and then, to the inexpressible relief of the bystanders, their meaning seemed to soak into the bewildered brain; for the look of terror gradually gave place to an expression of weary peace, and closing his eyes Brother Petroc fell asleep.

"Thank God," said the Abbot and Subprior together and for a moment they stood watching the sleeping man.

"I should like to move him asleep, if I can manage it," said the Subprior.

"He had better be taken to my room; it is on the ground floor," answered the Abbot.

---

[*] "Do not fear, we are friends, God has cured you."

"It is impossible to get absolute silence on the ground floor," was the response; "we cannot stop all the work of the house indefinitely. And your room, from that point of view, would be the very worst place in the world. People will always be forgetting and knocking at the door. This poor boy's mind is in such a state that, unless he gradually recovers, in perfect quiet, we might as well send for a taxi and take him to the Asylum straight away. It is risky to carry him upstairs, but more risky to leave him down. The room at the end of the Infirmary passage would be simply ideal, away from everybody and facing the sea. The only difficulty is getting him there. I think, however, if we could improvise a stretcher of a thin mattress on a strong curtain, we might manage it. At any rate it is worth trying."

The Abbot agreed; so the Brother with them was sent for another strong Lay Brother to act as fourth stretcher-bearer, and between them they brought the necessary things. They fetched a table and put it beside the niche, placed their improvised stretcher on the table; then, very carefully slipping the Abbot's cowl under the sleeping man they slowly drew him on to it. But as they moved him he began to stir a little.

"This will never do," said the Subprior. "we are living a nightmare tonight, and since taking risks seems the normal course to pursue, here goes for another." And tipping two or three drops from a phial into a small quantity of water he tilted the sleeping man's head a little, carefully poured the dose between the parted lips and watched the muscles of the throat relax.

"That will do," he said and turned around.

The second Lay Brother was holding close conference with the Abbot and the Infirmarians.

"Brother Peter says we shall never manage to carry the sick man upstairs on that mattress," said the former.

"No means of keeping him steady," added Brother Peter, by way of explanation.

"Then I'm done," said the Subprior with a shrug; "I can think of absolutely no other way of doing it."

"What about this coffin Father Procurator has here, in case it was needed when we shifted the graves," said Brother Peter, suddenly inspired. "This young man is not tall, so he would fit in quite nicely and we could carry him as steady as a rock."

The Subprior made a very wry face. It seemed a ghastly idea to restore a man to life and then carry him away in a coffin. However this really did seem the only solution; so they lifted the coffin on two stools beside the table and lowered Brother Petroc into it.

The journey to the room upstairs was very slow and tedious, but at last it was safely accomplished. The Lay Brother had bethought himself of getting someone to put hot bottles in the bed and leave a can full of hot water on the washstand, so that as soon as they reached the room the Abbot and Brother Peter were able to leave the two Infirmarians in full possession and go downstairs.

The next matter was to assemble the Community in the Chapter House, so that the Abbot might speak to them briefly on the subject of paramount interest to all.

"My Brethren," he said, "we have all witnessed tonight a most extraordinary occurrence, which has given us a new Brother. The only possible explanation seems to be that God has preserved this Brother Petroc's life by a miracle, until his own Brethren came back to his Abbey. God never acts without good reason, and we shall be shown in His own time what the reason for this miracle may be, as far as the knowledge may be necessary or profitable. Our part must be to wait quietly and in silence for a further manifestation of His will in this matter. At present we can do nothing but endeavor to foster the life so miraculously preserved.

"But there is one thing which must at all costs be avoided. If this tale gets outside the

Monastery, both our new Brother and ourselves will be exposed to all kinds of distraction and vexation. Visitors will flock to the place to see this nine days' wonder, and our life of prayer will be bound in consequence to suffer. So for his sake and also for ours, I ask you most emphatically to allow no word of tonight's occurrence ever to pass beyond these walls. It is our secret, and our secret it must remain. I will do all that is necessary, by writing the Bishop full details at once. No one else need know.

"A further point. It is quite possible, I might almost say probable, that this poor Brother's mind will never recover this evening's shock; in any case it will be a long business, requiring the most skilful treatment that Father Subprior can give. We can help in one way only and that is by avoiding all disturbance of the sick man. I therefore utterly forbid anyone to visit Brother Petroc, or even to go to the end of the Infirmary corridor where his cell is, without the express invitation of Father Subprior. I need hardly commend our new Brother to your prayers. It is already somewhat late, so we will go straight to Compline, and I ask for Brother Petroc and his nurses a special remembrance in our evening prayer."

Chapter Three

The Abbot was finding it far from easy to deal with his Subprior; in fact he was actually driven to pray for patience, which was a virtue that Father Abbot did not often need to pray about.

The morning after the discovery of Brother Petroc, the Subprior came, very much the medical man, to make his report. His patient had slept for two or three hours and then had wakened. He was for a time terrified and confused, though this had been apparently caused rather by a vague feeling of strangeness than by any definite realization of his whereabouts or condition. He had spoken

English, and though it had been quite unintelligible at first, the Subprior began after a while to grow more familiar with the change of intonation and accent and had even begun to understand odd words, here and there. In time it should become quite easy to use English as a means of communication. Last night however he had had recourse to Latin, and by its means he had been able to persuade Petroc to take nourishment several times. He had soothed the sick man with Psalms; for the familiar words seemed to give him a sense of security. Each time he had wakened the symptoms of terror had reappeared, though in a less marked degree. By morning he even appeared to recognize his nurse and to show signs of trust and confidence in him. There seemed every hope that in time and with care the brain would adjust itself to a proximation of the normal at least. But now what was Father Abbot going to do in the matter? Such a case had never before been known to medical science. The Subprior had no hesitation in saying that unless he had seen it with his own eyes he would simply have laughed at this tale of all vital functions suspended for something like four hundred years. But well-attested facts were stubborn things, and this one would revolutionize the whole outlook of medical science. Who knew to what discoveries it might not lead? In any case the matter ought to be followed up. He for his part would suggest sending for two or three of the best medical men of the day, with at least one brain specialist among them. The Abbot hardly seemed to realize the enormous importance of the whole case. Nothing so interesting happened once in a hundred years. It was a chance in a million.

The Abbot waited until the Subprior had talked himself out, then he said quietly:

"I have no intention whatever, Father, of sacrificing either Brother Petroc or ourselves on the Altar of Medical Science. Any possible gain in that direction would be more than counterbalanced by the loss the spiritual life of the Community would suffer if this house were made a centre of excitement and commotion. You have all the skill and knowledge necessary to deal with the case, which will be left entirely in your hands. I do not see how consultations and specialists will be more efficacious in restoring Brother Petroc to health than peace and calmness in the care of his own Brethren. After all, it is his right to live among us as one of ourselves. So I shall tell the Bishop, but absolutely no one else. As for explanation, the simplest and safest seems to me to accept the whole thing as a miracle."

This last sentence fairly set a match to the Subprior's wrath. Facts were awkward things, he knew, and the consequences of this one might very probably be difficult to deal with. But to call it a miracle was simply to use an inadequate explanation, in order to shelve the responsibility of facing it.

This was no restoration of a dead man to health and strength. For some reason which was not yet understood, a faint spark of life had been preserved in a man who had apparently fallen into a trance some four hundred years ago. The Subprior had used every means he could think of to preserve and strengthen this vital spark; but the result of his efforts was still extremely doubtful. His patient's state, both mental and physical, still gave cause for very grave anxiety. If the sick man upstairs were an instance of a miracle, he must readjust all his ideas. And so on.

At length the Abbot put an end to the monologue.

"If miracles are an interference with the laws of nature, then last night's occurrence is the continuation of an undoubted miracle which has lasted four hundred years. The fact that the completion of the work is in a great measure left in our hands has nothing to do with the matter. I am fully determined that no wind of this affair shall get outside the Monastery. Your business is to do your best to forward Brother Petroc's complete recovery. The rest you will kindly leave alone."

The Subprior, an excellent monk, ceased to argue, signed his obedience and left the room. But he did feel that life was undoubtedly hard. He was even now more interested in his old profession than he realized. It would have been such a joy and triumph to have contributed his quota, even though a monk, to the sum of medical knowledge. Like S. Peter he had left all things to follow Christ; and now when the hundred-fold promised, even in this life, had seemed just within his grasp, he had been forbidden to stretch out a hand to take it.

It speaks well for his virtue that he gave Brother Petroc much more than mere duty demanded; for he racked his brains to devise means of being of service to mind or body. And he had his reward, though for a long time he did not realize it, in the devoted love for Brother Petroc which grew up in his heart. For true love is only born of sacrifice, and the Subprior had never really loved before.

The days went by, and strength gradually returned to the sick man. He soon learnt to recognize the Abbot and Subprior, and gradually each began to understand the other's speech. But the bewildered look never left Petroc's face, and he seemed too apathetic to evince any curiosity as to his whereabouts, or concerning the events which had led to his present condition.

So the weeks passed and at last Brother Petroc was able to dress and walk about his cell a little. He spent hours at the window-seat, looking dreamily out and watching the gulls fish in the restless Atlantic just below him. But he scarcely spoke, save in courteous acknowledgement of some service, and he asked no questions.

If there were to be any question of complete mental recovery it would be necessary to find some means of rousing him, and the Subprior racked his brains for some way by which he could dispel the apathy which was holding his patient back. He happened one day to be in the Library looking up some references, when his glance chanced to rest on a glass case on the center table, in which among other treasures was an illuminated *Book of Hours*. It must have belonged to the former owners of the place, for the monks had come across it when clearing out a cupboard in the early days of their occupation of S. Brioc's. The Subprior pounced on it, for here was a connection with his patient's former life which might possibly effect the change he so much desired.

"Will you lend me this to show Brother Petroc?" he begged the Librarian. "I can't persuade him to show an interest in anything and here is something which will quite possibly bring back his memory and rouse him up to ask questions. Until we can find some sort of a stimulus his recovery is at a standstill."

"It is more his than ours," answered the Librarian, "so take it and welcome as far as I am concerned. Only have the kindness to mention the matter to Father Abbot before you show the book to Petroc."

The Subprior carried his treasure away, and the Abbot having willingly acceded his permission, he slipped quietly into Petroc's cell, laid the book on the table and went out. Petroc, sitting as usual listless on the window-seat, did not appear to see or hear him.

When he returned an hour later he was both horrified and relieved to find Brother Petroc on his knees by the table, with his head resting on his folded arms, crying his very soul out. The Subprior waited in silence until his grief had spent itself, and then, pushing him into a big chair, set about administering restoratives. But Petroc would have none of them, for at last his halting tongue was loosed, and he poured out a flood of agonized questions. He knew that book; once he had prayed from it. How did it come there? Where was he? What had happened to him? For God's sake would someone explain?

"If you will steady yourself and drink this brandy, I will send the Lay Brother for the Abbot, who will try to explain to you. But unless you are quite quiet and obedient I shall do nothing. I do want to rouse you, man, but if I kill you instead it will not suit me at all. Now steady! Pull yourself together! Things are hard for you, I know, but you've got plenty of self-control."

Brother Petroc obediently drank the brandy and sat quite still with his hands gripping the arms of his chair, while the Subprior sent for the Abbot.

The latter came quickly and drawing a chair close to Brother Petroc said very slowly and distinctly:

"Listen to me, Brother. For some wise reason of His own, God has kept you alive for four hundred years. You were buried on the eve of your ordination day, but you were not really dead. God preserved your life and you slept in peace until we found you in your grave. You are still in your old Monastery among your own Brethren who are only too pleased to welcome their new Brother. Your supposed death happened nearly four hundred years ago, but try not to dwell on that side of the matter; only remember you are still among Benedictines, and that God has work for which He has preserved you. So trust Him, be patient and obedient to Father Subprior, and try to get strong, for God will surely show you His Will."

The Abbot rose, blessed the Brother and slipped out of the cell.

Petroc's hands were white with pressure on the chair-arms and his face was set, but he said no word and quietly allowed the Subprior to put him to bed. That night he was again alarmingly ill. The apathy which had possess him had given place to high fever. All night long he tossed and muttered; the only words which were intelligible to the Subprior were "promise," and "paying the price," and these occurred over and over again. The Subprior watched by him and gave him everything he dared to bring down the temperature. At last, towards morning, the fever abated and the patient lay quiet. For a long time he lay very still with closed eyes, though his set lips forbade the

Subprior to hope that he slept. In the newly awakened mind some struggle was evidently going on, though the will was suppressing all outward manifestation. The Subprior could only watch and pray.

At last Petroc turned quite suddenly to the table by his bed and took up the Crucifix lying there. Very slowly he kissed each of the Five Wounds and then laid the Crucifix down again. There was a short pause; then he turned to the Subprior at his side:

"Father," he said, "will you have the great kindness to tell Father Abbot that if he will, of his charity, receive the new Subject God has sent him, I will do my best to be his humble obedient son."

He turned on his side and fell quietly asleep. When he awoke his mind woke also. For some time it worked lowly and with effort, but it was really working. Brother Petroc was fully alive and ready to carry out God's Will.

The Subprior carried his patient's message to the Abbot and reported his very evident improvement, but he said very little else. The only Person he really spoke to on the subject was God Almighty, and to Him he said:

"I humbly acknowledge the preservation of Brother Petroc's life and reason to be a miracle,"—this was his Act of Faith—then he continued: "I was a fool ever to think otherwise. I might have known that the Abbot was infinitely wiser about such matters than I,"—this was his Act of Humility and Contrition.—"And if Brother Petroc does not grudge the heavy price he has to pay for something he evidently covets, the least I can do is to give the small exchange I have offered for my vocation, without grumbling over it, or giving the bare minimum."

Then he went off to the Brother Infirmarian to help him concoct a wonderful breakfast that might not look too unfamiliar to Brother Petroc and might tempt him to an appetite.

Chapter Four

When Sunday came, the Subprior decided on trying another experiment. Some fifteen minutes before the Sung Mass he took Brother Petroc down the passage to the tribune for the sick. This was a gallery which stretched across the west end of the Choir, just above the public church. The Monks' Choir ran the length of the Cloister, and the Church had been enlarged by knocking down part of the west wall and building an annex with a roof somewhat lower than the rest of the building. The tribune of the sick was at the junction of the old and new building, and its floor was the roof of the public church, so that anyone kneeling there could see the Altar and Choir, while the public church was out of sight.

The Subprior made Petroc comfortable in a corner at the front with a prie-dieu and an easy chair; then he slipped to the back, where he could watch his patient without disturbing him. Petroc knelt down and looked around, at first, in some bewilderment; later, as he caught sight of different familiar objects, memory began to waken. He looked at the stalls and the monks kneeling there; he glanced up at the organ in the gallery at the side. Then his eye caught the High Altar. He knit his brows and looked thoughtful. Then his gaze rested for a moment on the Sanctuary Lamp. There was a stifled cry. "My Lord and my God!" said Petroc, and pulling his hood over his head he covered his face with his hands.

He was roused by the Organist intoning the *Asperges*, and raising his head, smiled as one who recognizes an old and familiar friend. From that moment he was alive to every sound and movement going on below. The expression of patient apathy so often visible on his face had given place to one of almost painful attention. At one time he smiled, as one who experiences some great and unexpected joy, and even as he smiled the tears ran down his cheeks. With rapt attention he followed every step of the Great Sacrifice to its close. But when the Subprior came to summon him, after the Celebrant and his Assistants had left the Altar, he was unable to stand alone, and had to be almost carried back to his cell. The bed was pulled under the open window and he was laid on it. He did not speak again of his own accord that day; but there was no lack of life and feeling now in the still face with its closed eyes.

Next morning when the Lay Brother came with his dinner, he was missing. Much perturbed, the Brother hastened to the Subprior with the news. The Subprior considered for a moment and then went upstairs to the tribune of the sick. There knelt Brother Petroc, absorbed in prayer.

That afternoon the Subprior went to the Abbot's room.

"Brother Petroc is making wonderful progress," he said. "He will soon begin to wander about and ask questions. The monks had better be told to answer him if he speaks, but to volunteer nothing. If he begins to enquire about his past life they must refer him to you."

A few days later the Sacristan found Petroc in the Choir, walking round and handling stalls and lectern with a rapt expression. He left the Brother alone and busied himself in another part of the Choir. Presently he felt a touch on his arm.

"I think there was once a statue of Our Lady, just here," said Petroc. The Sacristan had never heard him speak before, so he had to repeat his remark twice before it was understood.

"We moved it here into this chapel when the Church was enlarged," he answered, leading the way.

When they reached the arch he just stopped and pointed to the statue, then walked away leaving Petroc gazing with upturned face at the image of his Mother.

The Community was beginning to get used to the sight of Brother Petroc gliding like a shadow about the house; but even the Abbot received something of a shock, a few days later, to find him at Vespers, standing in the stall of the youngest professed monk with the old *Book of Hours* in his hand. After that he came regularly to Vespers and Compline and would have done more, only the Subprior forbade.

One day the Abbot came to his cell and found Brother Petroc studying a book of engravings after the old masters that the Subprior had lent him. He was poring over a copy of Leonardo da Vinci's Last Supper.

"It is wonderful, Brother" said the Abbot, "to think that every day that Act is renewed; and every day, if we will, we may share in that Sacred Banquet."

"It is good to be a priest," answered Petroc; "we others must wait for the great feasts."

"Not nowadays," said the Abbot. "About twenty-five years ago the Pope issued an Encyclical recommending frequent and daily Communion. You can go every day if you like. What about making a beginning tomorrow?"

Petroc's eyes shone; then his face clouded over.

"There is Confession to be considered, Father Abbot. I am not like the rest of you. I cannot remember when I last went, nor what I said. I should need to think carefully and my brain does not work easily yet."

"Come here, Brother," said the Abbot with a smile, crossing to the window-seat. He made Petroc sit down beside him, helped him to examine his conscience and then gave him Absolution.

Next morning he himself brought Petroc Holy Communion. They thought he would have died of joy, and it was far on in the evening before the Subprior breathed freely again. Brother Petroc's hold on the thread of life was still a very slight one. After that however Holy Communion was brought to him every day and with the Sacrament strength seemed to flow in.

It was not long after this that the Brother began to grow restless. He would slip downstairs and wander round the cloister garth, then he would go upstairs again and along to the tribune for the sick, then down again and out into the garden. The Subprior, watching him closely, came to the conclusion that it was time to make another forward step. So he went to the Abbot and suggested that the latter should pay a surprise visit to Brother Petroc's cell that evening in order to discover, if possible, what was troubling him.

The Abbot agreed, and accordingly slipped up after supper, to find Petroc on the window-seat watching the gulls with a very abstracted air.

"It's a beautiful evening, Brother," he said, "and by the look of the sunset we shall have a fine day tomorrow."

"Yes, Father Abbot," answered Petroc, and fell to playing with the cord which moved the upper sash of the window.

"I was one of three brothers—the youngest," Brother Petroc was addressing the setting sun, slowly and with effort, as though he were searching some very deep recess of his memory. "We were the Trelants of Penruddock—a small estate—some twenty miles from here. Folk said we were an ancient race—I know we were a poor one. In the chapel in the house was an old wooden statue of the Blessed Mother of God. Our tradition said that long ago—in the time of the Confessor—pirates had landed hereabouts and made a raid on the house of my forebears. They were repulsed—so in revenge they went into a small chapel—just outside the village—took the statue of God's Mother—to whom the village was dedicated, and threw it into a bonfire they made on the cliff. Petroc Trelant was at Polgarth when the raid took place—and on his way home—catching sight of the pirates—hid behind a gorse bush. But when he saw them fling the image in the fire—he could no longer remain in hiding—for the Trelants are ever devout to God's Blessed Mother—so he rushed out, leaped into the flames, and lifted out the statue. 'Tis said the pirates were so amazed that they made no attempt to get him—'Tis also said—that as he carried the statue home in his blistered arms—he heard the voice of God's Mother promising—that there should never fail a priest to the house of Trelant—as long as the name should last. Be that as it may—there has never been a time in the memory of man—when there was no priest of the family.

"My father, therefore, was greatly rejoiced when I—a little lad only nine years of age—made up my mind to enter the Abbey here. I came at once, and was very happy. But times soon grew difficult—the Bishop of Exeter was a Schismatic and we had to obtain leave from the Pope for our Abbot to ordain his own monks. Therefore I was seven and twenty years old—in May I think it was—before the time came when I could be ordained. The date fixed was August 15th—and about a month previously—my two brothers went to join Humphrey Arundell, when he marched into Devon—to restore God's religion by the sword. It was on August 12th—if I make no mistake—that a messenger came from my father to say that both my brothers had been slain in the skirmish when Sir Humphrey took Launceston. I remember thinking, as I walked in the garden, in a maze of sorrow, that now there remained but me in whom Our Lady could fulfill her promise. Then I bethought me of going to the chapel to remind her that she had never been known to fail in her word. After that I know no more, until that dim, strange time, when I lay here abed, while Father Subprior ministered to me. Then I found on the table here my old *Book of Hours*, and you told me my story was nigh four hundred years old. Is there no way to piece the tale?"

The Abbot shifted a little and moved his gaze from the monk's face to the fast purpling twilight.

Then he too began to speak slowly into the young night.

"Brother Petroc, in fulfillment of Our Lady's promise, was to be ordained on August 15th. On August 6th the Cornishmen were defeated at S. Mary's Clyst. The band from S. Brioc must have been almost destroyed there, because on August 12th the Abbot appeared to have received news of the return of the remnant, pursued by a band of King's soldiers. We conclude this from the paper found in your grave, which says that a band of soldiers was approaching the Monastery, hence the flight to Long Island. Now the siege of Exeter was not raised until a few days later and the decisive battle at Sampford Courtney was not until August 17th, after which the Cornishmen fell back on Launceston. So that the S. Brioc's men must have made a separate retreat followed by a detachment of the main army. At the very time when this news reached the Abbey, Brother Petroc must have fallen ill and become insensible. The paper found on his body says that he was buried in haste for the Community were leaving the Abbey at once. The tale in the village is that the monks went to Long Island and the villagers fled. Later, on their return, they went to the island to bring help to the monks. They found traces of their occupation and the wreckage of their boats, but they found no living soul; which proves that every one had died of starvation or drowning. If Brother Petroc had remained in his normal health and strength, he would never have been ordained. But Our Lady never fails of her promise, so she sent him a sleep which lasted until his own Brethren came back to wake him. Now it only remains for them to see to the carrying out of Our Lady's wish."

There was absolute silence for quite five minutes after the Abbot had ceased speaking. Then the younger monk turned.

"I am a puzzled man, Father Abbot. My mind finds it a constant struggle to connect the two portions of a life suspended for nigh four hundred years. Will you be patient with me while I grapple with the tale we have completed tonight? Then I promise to try to forget the past and live in the present. Only God is great enough to reward you and my Brethren for all you have done."

The Abbot rose in silence, and in silence the young monk knelt for his blessing. In the corridor outside he found the Subprior pacing restlessly up and down; he dreaded the effect on Brother Petroc of each new revelation, yet it was absolutely necessary to enlighten him.

"He has taken the story very well and is quite quiet and natural," the Abbot assured him. "He is certainly a very brave man. If I were you I should leave him entirely to himself tonight. If he does not go to bed there will be no great harm done. He is struggling to make a connected whole of his life, past and present. Until that is done he cannot settle down, and we shall have no further progress. Thank God that in this extraordinary and difficult situation we have to deal with a young man blessed with Elizabethan nerves.

Twentieth-century neurasthenia would never stand it."

"I am willing to grant the Elizabethan nerves, Father," responded the Subprior a trifle testily, "but I also postulate an Elizabethan heart. And let me tell you that a heart four hundred years old will not stand playing with. However, if he is quiet he will probably come to no harm, and any disturbance might just upset some delicate adjustment necessary to his recovery."

And he followed his Superior downstairs to Compline.

Chapter Five

Brother Petroc kept his cell for a day or two after his conversation with the Abbot. Then he accosted the Lay Brother who came to take away his breakfast.

"Will you please show me the way to Father Abbot's room?" he asked. "I would have speech with him."

So the Brother took Petroc downstairs and showed him the door, instructing him to knock and wait for an answer. The Abbot was disengaged, so Petroc's knock received an immediate response. He opened the door, crossed the room quickly and knelt at the Abbot's feet.

"The past is now buried, Father Abbot, and I am ready to learn how to live in the present."

"I am very glad indeed to hear this, Brother. Tomorrow then you may begin to come to the refectory for your meals, and follow as much of the regular life as Father Subprior will allow. But remember you are under obedience to him. Ask him to explain our refectory customs to you, and whatever else you may need as occasion arises. I will speak to the Novice Master, for I think you would find it helpful if the Novices took their midday recreation with you, in turns, and tried to give you some idea of the changes which have taken place during the last four hundred years."

Then it was that the Abbot, for the first time, saw Petroc smile in genuine amusement. It was a Cornishman's smile beginning in the eyes and travelling slowly to the lips.

"That will occupy them more than a little," he said.

"Later on we will begin to talk about studies. Some revision work, at least, will be necessary before ordination. But for the present your business is to get strong. Your education, until you are quite robust, we will leave in the hands of the Novices. God bless you, Brother!"

Brother Petroc was determined to live up to his promise, so without loss of time he went in search of the Subprior. The latter listened to his tale, secretly admired his courage and sympathized openly with his desire for ordination. But his attitude with regard to regular life was somewhat uncompromising, for he arranged an horary in which rest and quiet played a considerable part; and he specially insisted on complete relaxation after the hour spent with the Novices.

"You will be dizzy and longing for peace, after you have listened to an hour's exposition from one of those young men," he said. "remember they will be thrilled to tell you things, and will quite forget how strange and puzzling much of it will be to you," for the Subprior's medical knowledge enabled him to realize as no one else did the exceeding delicacy of constitution which was the result of Petroc's long trance; and also how great a physical and mental strain was entailed by the effort to adapt himself to his new life. Besides, his charge had grown to be the apple of his eye, and he dreaded the possible result of fresh shocks.

But Brother Petroc himself seemed to have begun a new lease of life. He went to Choir and refectory with the rest, and began to find various small ways of making himself useful. The hour of his instruction by the Novices, however, was the time when he showed himself most interested and alert.

There had been considerable excitement in the Novitiate when their Master had explained to his charges, three guileless, open-hearted young men, what were the Abbot's wishes. When he had given his message, he wisely dispensed silence for an hour or so, that they might discuss their new duties. They took their responsibilities very seriously and set about drawing up a plan of studies, in which each was assigned a different part. Brother Gregory the youngest was given History, on the ground that being last at school he had probably forgotten least; Brother Pius was to deal with Geography and Economics; while Brother Leo was to endeavor to give their pupil an idea of modern life and modern inventions. Brother Gregory and Brother Pius gave their instructions in the garden if fine, in the Novitiate library if wet or cold, and found the work fairly plain-sailing; but Brother Leo was breaking fresh ground altogether. He began by showing his pupil pictures of modern thoroughfares, engines, motor cars, aeroplanes, ships, bicycles, factories and machinery. Then he brought drawings of parts of machinery and explained principles and details. Next he took him to the side of the cliff overlooking the high road, so that from a safe distance he might get some idea of traffic. Finally, on one holiday afternoon, he got leave for the other two to join him and together they took

Petroc by easy stages to the cutting just outside Polgarth station and for a breathless hour they studied trains. The final triumph of the afternoon however was to find the quarry quiet and the engine-man at leisure, so that he could explain the mechanism of the little donkey engine that worked the machinery.

Still, if Brother Petroc was deeply interested in the new world opened out to him, his instructors, as the Abbot had probably foreseen, benefited even more than their pupil. They had never before been in touch with such a mind, keen, incisive and enquiring. Any statement they might make was taken up and carried through to its logical conclusion, with a swiftness and accuracy that amazed them. Often enough a careless, slipshod statement, questioned by Petroc, landed them in a maze of difficulty and contradiction from which they were totally unable to extricate themselves; then their pupil would come to the rescue and a few sentences would make all clear again. He would apologize sometimes for what he had done, saying that it was how he had been trained and he was sorry this habit of his gave them trouble. His questions were short and absolutely to the point; his own answers were a model of clear conciseness.

Yet—and this moved the Novices to wonder—this logical, clear-headed man possessed a passionate love of beauty in any form, and he taught them to use ears and eyes in a way they had never done before, impressing on them that beauty is, after all, only a most gracious expression of truth. But in spite of the cultured intelligence and the fine lawyer-like mind, which was regaining its strength with wonderful speed, Brother Petroc possessed withal so disarming a fund of humility that his instructors were not galled when over and over again they were proved out of their own mouths to have made fools of themselves. He was so utterly unconscious of having shown either his own superior intelligence or his teachers' carelessness of thought and expression that he gave them no reason to feel ashamed. His slow speech was so weighted with courteous humility that even the most sensitive could not feel abashed.

The Novice Master was delighted with the mental progress made by his pupils after a few months' intercourse with Brother Petroc. The Subprior was delighted with the progress his patient was making, and began to shape plans for the future. The Abbot looked on completely satisfied with the result of his experiment.

So the weeks slipped quietly by and in the surprising way in which it always happens the Community suddenly found Advent, with its trumpet-cry *"Ecce venit Rex!"* was upon them, and Christmas loomed ahead. The Novices were sitting at recreation in their Common-room one evening when the conversation turned on the subject of the approaching feast.

"I wonder what Christmas will feel like to Brother Petroc?" said Brother Leo. "Of course I know that the essence of the feast is always the same and nothing can touch that; but there are what you might call the extras—parcels, letters from home and the rest of it. I should think that side of the feast might come pretty hard on him."

"I wonder if we could do anything," said Brother Gregory. "Do you think, Father Master, we should be allowed to ask him to spend Christmas and the next two or three days up here with us? Then he could be our guest of honor, and perhaps he won't remember how lonely he really is."

"That will rest with Father Abbot of course," replied the Novice Master; "But I will certainly ask him. He can but say no. For my part, the more you young men see of Brother Petroc the better I am pleased. He's making you think in a way I have never been able to."

The Subprior happened to be with the Abbot when the Novice Master came to bring his charges' request.

"What do you think about it, Father?" asked the Abbot.

"I should be simply delighted," was the answer. "I have been considering the question of Christmas lately and rather dreading its possible effect on my patient. Christmas was even more of a family feast in his day than it is now."

"As Father Subprior approves," the Abbot smiled at the Novice Master, "for you know he is very despotic as far as Brother Petroc is concerned, please tell your young men that I shall be very pleased for them to invite their pupil to the Novitiate for Christmas and that I trust them to give him a really happy feast."

So the Novices sent an invitation to Brother Petroc, which was accepted in due form in their pupil's best hand and characteristic spelling. After High Mass on Christmas Day he made his way to the Novices' quarters and was received with great honor. For three days he shared their life as one of themselves and then went back to the Community.

On the evening after Petroc's departure, the Novices were again at recreation and the conversation turned as a matter of course on their visitor.

"I've never spent such a Christmas nor seen such a man," said Brother Pius. "He was alive to everything and took the deepest interest in all we said or did. But now I come to think of it, did you fellows notice that he never once spoke of himself? He must have spent far different and much more thrilling Christmases in those old days, but he never said a word of his own experiences. One quite forgot, somehow, that he was a stranger and a visitor; he seemed so much one of ourselves. Of course I know that he is really holy, it's in his face, somehow. But don't you think, Father Master, that those sixteenth-century chaps always seemed far more interested in what they were doing than in their own personality?"

"People were much more objective in their outlook and took a simpler view of life. Luther and the other leaders of the Reformation did great harm to Europe, beyond their actual heresy, in teaching people to regard themselves as the central point of their own universe. Nearly all the earlier heresies were connected with some dogma concerning God or Our Lady, and reacted indirectly on the lives of the heretics; for instance, the excesses of the Alibgenses followed from their notion of two First Principles, one good and one evil. When we come to the Reformation however we find the leaders attacking the human personality directly; Luther belittled man's responsibility for his actions by his doctrine of justification by faith alone; Calvin attacked free-will by his heresy regarding predestination. This drew people's attention to themselves in a way that it had never been drawn before, and the habit of introspection has continued to grow. Hence you find a good deal of unselfishness in the world, but very little selflessness. If Brother Petroc had been born fifty years later, or born when he was, in some centre of intellectual activity, you would have found a very different man, much more like what we are now. As it is, you are in contact with a survival of the ages of faith, the great ages of the world, and this is what you find so unusual and interesting. Added to this, Brother Petroc has undoubtedly been very close to God all his life, so you see nothing of the other side of the same picture: a coarseness and a certain robustness which you would have found to grate."

"That is the reason why Brother Petroc is so fine then, Father Master?"

"Yes, Brother Leo, I fancy it is. And that is the reason why I am so pleased for you lads to come in contact with him."

A few days later a friend living in the town offered the monks the loan of his wireless set for a week. It happened that week that there was a programme which the monks would find interesting and useful, so the Abbot, though he resolutely set his face against a permanent installation in the Monastery, accepted the loan with gratitude.

On the first afternoon the monks gathered together in the Common-room to hear a celebrated choir render a Plain Chant Mass. The Abbot was next the Prior at one end of the room and, a little apart, the Subprior was sitting alone; he was not particularly interested in music, so he was amusing himself by watching its effect in the faces of his Brethren. Presently the door opened and Petroc walked in. The Subprior half rose; with a shock of dismay he suddenly remembered that he had not mentioned the wireless to his patient. For a moment Petroc stared in utter bewilderment at the room, full of sound but empty of singers; the bewilderment gave place to an expression of fear. Then the monk straightened himself, looked round the room, and seated himself near to the door, still watching the faces of the others.

One of the older monks, a clever, cultured man, caught sight of Petroc presently, crossed the room and took a chair at his side. Very quietly he began to speak to his companion, evidently explaining matters, for he took a notebook out of his pocket and began to draw diagrams. Petroc seemed to be following what he said, for from time to time he gave little motions of assent and two or three times appeared to volunteer a remark. His duties called the Subprior away presently, and as he went out he saw that Petroc and his companion were still engaged in an earnest whispered conversation. That evening he went to Petroc's cell to learn his impressions, and incidentally gained an unexpected insight into his outlook and character.

"What did you think of the wireless concert this afternoon?" he enquired.

Petroc smiled a little.

"I came," he said, "into a room filled with the sound of chanting monks. At first I supposed it was our Brethren and I looked round. Then I saw that they were sitting silent, so I knew it was not they. My next thought was that there was something preternatural and a motion of fear invaded my mind. But Father Abbot and the rest appeared so unmoved that I perceived it to be some natural phenomenon beyond my ken, so I sat me down and tried to keep wonderment at bay. Then Dom Placid took pity on my ignorance and gave me an exposition of the principles of this strange contrivance."

"You appeared to understand what he was talking about?"

"I had played the harp in my boyhood and was therefore not unacquainted with the effects of vibration; from that he managed to give me some elementary idea of what was happening."

"It must have been a stupendous thing for you to imagine this annihilation of distance—" began the Subprior, but stopped suddenly as Petroc with a scared face held up a warning hand.

"Hush, Father, thus I must never think!"

"I am sorry, Brother, but to me that would be the first impression."

"Truly, Father, you people of this present age use every faculty indiscriminately. Therefore, if you will pardon me, were you in my place you would incontinently go mad. Now I have been taught to separate the action of my faculties. Therefore in trying to understand what I may of my present life and its ways, as far as possible I use reason alone. Thus I may follow a chain of reasoning and understand dimly how some of these marvels happen. But I take it as in the old days we learnt to follow a thesis. As for anything further I dare not."

"Um-m. You are quite right. It is the only thing to do, and any of us muddle-headed moderns would certainly fail and go mad. But what do you do with your imagination, Brother?"

"When I was a small child, Father, mine own father took me in front of him on horse-back to see a morality play. I remember naught save that I watched the players, imps and virtues, as it might be an ever-changing picture, understanding little but amused by the bright colors and antics of the players. Some years later I went again. This time I was able to follow the motion of the play. Now it seemeth to me that I am again a very little child, in the arms of my Heavenly Father, watching a pageant. I understand little and I ask as little as may be, but am content to watch the show in His

Arms. If at times I grow weary or affrighted then do I turn my eyes away and hide my face on His Shoulder until the terror has passed. And I ever pray 'Lord in Thy Mercy let nothing come too close nor seem too real.' Thus I can turn my reason alone on what I am told, holding with heart and imagination tight to my Heavenly Father."

The Subprior drew a long breath and stared at his companion for a second or two; then he said very slowly and gently:

"What would happen, Brother, should duty or obedience bring you in close touch with the world and its doings?'"

"That I sometimes fear, Father, for as I see it now, if I am drawn into contact with the world, so that imagination must needs be used, then shall I go mad or die. 'Twould be like plunging into a raging current and being whirled one knows not whither. But even so, if I begin to fear and sink as Peter did, surely the Hand of the Master would be stretched out to succor. So even thus will I trust."

Chapter Six

The Abbot and Subprior soon found out that Petroc counted it a real privilege to be allowed to take a share in the Community duties; but nothing gave him greater pleasure than to be sent to help the Sacristan. When that official on his side discovered that if he presented Petroc with a few flowers and two or three vases the result was such as to rejoice the heart of a lover of beauty, he used to coax him to arrange the Altars before a big feast.

It was February 1st, and Brother Petroc was busied in decking his Mother's statue in the Lady

Chapel, arranging small pots of snowdrops round her feet. The Altar itself, he had decided, should be arranged with Christmas roses, and he knew that the Mother would like her own statue to be dressed very simply, when it stood so close to the spot where her Son was coming down next day.

As he worked he became aware that he was not alone; someone was kneeling in the chapel behind him. Petroc had been well trained, so he continued his work without so much as glancing around.

Presently he discovered that he was short of two candles, which would necessitate a visit to the sacristy. As he came down the Altar steps he saw a woman kneeling at the rails. On his approach she rose and moved towards him. Now Petroc had never yet spoken to any save his own Brethren; he therefore felt no little dismay as the stranger came in his direction. However he could not turn back without discourtesy, and there was no other way out of the chapel, so he put the best face he could on the matter and held on his way.

"Father!" said the woman, and Petroc stopped. Her appearance somehow gave Petroc a disagreeable shock. She was young, she was beautiful, she was well and suitably dressed; but somehow and somewhere there was something very wrong. Her attitude was defiant, yet she seemed ill at ease. Her head was thrown well back and her arms hung quite stiff and rigid at her side. She did not seem to want to speak to Petroc, but to be doing so in spite of herself.

"I am sorry, Madam," answered Petroc with a little effort; "if you want a priest you will have to ask the Brother in the sacristy. I am not yet ordained."

"I don't want a priest, thank you," said the girl tartly; "I merely want to know what time Mass will be said here tomorrow."

The tone was so sharp and acrid that involuntarily Petroc looked up and caught her eyes watching him intently. With a little shudder he quickly lowered his, for he had never seen such a face, white and set like a mask, while the lips were compressed into a thin line and the eyes were cold and glittering as ice.

"The Mass at this Altar will be at half-past six," he answered, and then added almost in spite of himself, "Are you in trouble, Madam?"

"Trouble? Certainly not," said the girl, and there was a ring of defiance in her voice. "On the contrary I am on the eve of realizing both my greatest desire and my highest ambition—I have worked and struggled long enough for the one, and hesitated long enough before seizing the other."

"Your pardon, Madam," responded Petroc. "I will pray that you may be happy in the attainment of what you have desired and striven for so long."

His companion gave a little gasp; for one second a look of pain flashed across her face. Then she turned and walked quickly away, leaving Petroc oppressed with a vague sense of something wrong. He did not know why, but he was certain that the lady was in need of prayer. Well, he would do his best.

Meanwhile the Abbot was in the guest quarters engaged with a visitor. About twelve months before a widow and her only daughter had settled in S. Brioc. They seemed fairly well-to-do and were excellent Catholics, but they lived their own lives together and knew no one. Dom Maurus had visited them once or twice, but beyond that they had no connection with the Abbey. Mrs. Wheeler, the mother, had come up to see the Abbot this morning in great distress.

"My daughter has always been rather headstrong, Father Abbot, and for certain reasons I was obliged to let her pass the greater part of her childhood away from me, at school. But she has always been really good, as well as headstrong, and her religion has meant a great deal to her. The—" she hesitated—"The certain reasons I spoke about just now have obliged us to live a very quiet life, but Josie wished this herself and she has always seemed quite contented to be alone with me. In fact this sort of lonely life has been her own choice."

The Abbot nodded encouragingly.

"Have you—" Again Mrs. Wheeler hesitated. "I wonder if you have come across a man called Symes. Henry Symes, an artist who has settled down in one of the new bungalows beyond Lee Point. He stopped one day, when my daughter was sketching, to admire her work. I think she has a great gift for painting; and because of this common interest between them they became great friends. I could see that Josie was upset and unhappy. She has a strong nature, which she has always been obliged to suppress. A month ago the man asked her to marry him; and then I found out that he was divorced and his wife was still living."

Again the Abbot gave his encouraging little nod.

"When I told Josie, I naturally concluded that it would mean an end to the engagement. But to my surprise and horror she told me that she did not care, that his wife had behaved badly to him, and he was to be pitied. She said that she couldn't live without him, that they could be married in a Registry Office, and that she was certain it would be a marriage before God who knew the real facts of the case. I did all I could to shake her, but it was useless. They are to be married tomorrow quietly. The most extraordinary thing about the whole matter is that Josie has made up her mind to hear Our Lady's Mass first; though, of course, she knows she can't go to Holy Communion.

"What has completed her infatuation is the fact that this man is holding a private exhibition of his pictures in London next week, and has promised to exhibit some of hers among them. Her work is undoubtedly good, but she has been very unhappy because she could not get it noticed. However in this way she hopes to make a start. They mean to stay at his bungalow until he has to go up to superintend the hanging of his pictures, and then they will spend some weeks in London together. What ought I to do in the matter?"

The Abbot sat still for a few moments, considering; then he said:

"Your daughter used to be a really good girl?"

"Yes! She was a thoroughly practical Catholic and went to Communion every day. She was particularly devout to Our Lady, and I suppose she is going to her Mass tomorrow with some vague idea of getting her protection and securing her final Salvation in spite of the life she knows she is going to lead. I can only think, Father, that my poor girl's mind is somehow unhinged. Naturally speaking her affliction cut her off from all ideas of love and marriage, so I suppose when it really came into her life she allowed it to overmaster her sense of right."

"How shall you behave towards her after her marriage?"

"I have told her that I can't have her and her husband at my house or go to theirs. I have asked her to write to me sometimes, but—but I have explained that until she gives this man up—" The mother's voice failed her.

"I am exceedingly sorry for you," the Abbot said gently, "but I can offer you no further advice, for I really don't see what more you can do. Your only business, now, is to pray hard for your daughter and to try to make her realize that your home is always open to her as soon as she repents of her sin. Try to make repentance as easy as you can for her, but be sure also that she clearly understands how strongly you reprobate what she is doing. I will remember her specially in my Mass tomorrow. It is strange that I am saying the 6.30 at the Lady Altar, for her devotion to our Lady is a very strong influence in her favor. For the Blessed Mother takes special care of her children and has never been known to fail one who is devout to her."

"Thank you very much, Father. I will try to be patient and pray. I don't mind what happens if only my girl comes back to God."

The Abbot saw his visitor to the door and stood for a moment looking after her.

About a week later Petroc was again busy with his Altars. He was making remote preparations for the feast of Our Lady of Lourdes. For the Abbot had lent him a book all about the Grotto and its history, and Petroc had found something of a kindred spirit in Bernadette. As he moved about arranging and planning he suddenly remembered having seen some very early daffodils struggling into bloom in a sheltered corner of the copse, so he came down the Church, meaning to go out that way and examine the buds to see if by any possibility they would be ready by the 10th. As he came out of the Church door, he walked straight into the girl who had spoken to him in Church the previous week. He moved quickly to one side to let her pass, but she stood still, facing him resentfully. He found those intent eyes fixed on his face more than a little disconcerting.

"I wish you would leave me alone," she said in a sullen voice. Her intonation was peculiar, harsh and rather forced.

"I think you mistake me, Madam," answered Petroc. "I have only seen you once in my life and that was last week, when you asked me the hour of Mass at the Lady Altar." He wished that she would not stare so.

"I am making no mistake," answered the girl in the same sullen, reluctant tone. "You said then that you would pray for me and I haven't had a minute's peace since. You and your serene boy's face have been with me everywhere, disturbing my work, coming between me and my happiness, and reminding me of things I want to forget. I tell you I'm perfectly happy. I have got everything I wanted. I am going to London tomorrow with my husband, to help him to prepare an exhibition of his work and mine. Perfectly happy!" she added in her strange dead voice. "I don't want your prayers. I don't want your pity. All I want is to forget what I have been. So please leave me in peace and let me enjoy the first real happiness I have ever had."

She paused for breath and in that pause Brother Petroc slipped past her and turned through the enclosure gate which led to the Monastery garden. The girl was undoubtedly mad, or she would never have attacked him in that fashion. Petroc was not in the least afraid but the encounter had left a disagreeable question in his mind. Could his prayers really be an injury to anyone? And how could he, Petroc, present in the flesh in S. Brioc's Monastery, haunt an unknown woman in all her goings and comings?

On his way through the garden he met the Abbot returning from the little farm, whither the Procurator had taken him to inspect some young stock he wished to sell.

"Where are you off to in such a hurry, Brother?" he enquired of Petroc.

"There are a few daffodils in the little copse, by the farm," answered the monk. "I am going to see whether they will be in bloom for our Lady's feast."

"I believe that the flowers come up expressly for you, my son," said the Abbot; "you always seem to find them before anyone else is even thinking of looking for them. However, as I have ten minutes to spare, I am coming with you this time to see how you work your magic."

Petroc laughed and walked down beside the Abbot, who always seized any opportunity of making a break in the Brother's lonely life.

"As I came through the Church just now I suddenly came upon a woman who was most assuredly running lunatic," remarked the latter.

"A woman running lunatic? What do you mean precisely, Brother? In any case I suppose the Sacristan is in the Church in case of accidents?"

"Yes, Father Abbot, he was in the Sanctuary. Moreover, when I slipped past her, she turned and walked out of the gate."

"She stopped me as I came out of the Church door and told me to leave her alone. I answered that she was mistaken, for I had never seen her save once, when she asked me the hour of Our Lady's Mass next day. But she held to it that I disturbed her by my prayers; and indeed I had promised to pray for her, when she first spoke to me, for though she denied it she seemed in trouble. She went on to tell me that she had realized all her desires and ambitions and was going to London town to seen an exhibition of her own pictures and those of her husband. She said that I haunted her day and night, making her unhappy and bringing back memories for which she had no relish. I answered naught but slipped by and left her. Assuredly she is lunatic; for how could I, present here in the flesh, be also present in the spirit elsewhere? And though my poor prayers may do her no benefit, they surely will not be apt to harm."

By this time they had reached the clump of daffodils, and the Abbot made no immediate response to Petroc's questions. Instead he stooped down to examine the half-open buds and, as he looked, he thought rapidly.

'*Petroc's lunatic must be that unfortunate daughter of Mrs. Wheeler. She evidently refuses to own to herself that she has done wrong, but she finds Petroc, with his half unearthly look, disturbing to her conscience. She cannot be really quite sane just now, to speak to him as she did. He is so near to God that his prayers will be very efficacious and she is probably conscious of their power and does not want the grace they bring. He must certainly go on praying, but there will be no need to give him details which he will probably only half understand and which will only worry and distress him.*' Aloud he said:

"I think your daffodils will be ready. Pick them in good time and put them in tepid water; that will make them open. About the woman who spoke to you. I know something of her, and if she really is the one I mean, she is in the greatest need of prayer. You must pray as hard as you can; she probably does not like the thought of your doing so; it reminds her of something she will deeply regret having done, if she does not do so already. But continue, nevertheless. In regard to your haunting her, you of course know best whether or no you are really witch or pixie; otherwise, of course, it is only the memory of you and your prayers which disturbs her; and that is to her good."

"Neither witch nor pixie am I," answered Petroc, with a twinkle; then he added very earnestly, "but I will pray."

On the way back the Abbot questioned him as to his progress in his studies with the Novices. When they reached the Church, the Abbot turned into the Sacristy.

"Keep an eye on Brother Petroc," he said to the Sacristan, "and do not allow him to be disturbed or worried by outsiders. He is absolutely to be trusted, of course; but life, even in here, must be so difficult at times that I do not want him to have the extra strain that contact with the world outside will certainly bring."

Brother Petroc went to the Lady Chapel and there knelt down. He had a responsibility laid on him of praying for this unknown woman who needed prayers, though she did not like them. So he prayed a wordless prayer, one of those prayers whose content cannot be explained or the result measured. For when heart speaks to heart things may happen for which words are inadequate and all explanation too gross.

Lent drew on, and in its turn gave place to Easter, and still Brother Petroc throve. The Subprior who had been watching him narrowly was satisfied at last. So on Easter Monday he went down to the Abbot's room: "Brother Petroc has gained ground wonderfully, Father; the improvement he has shown during the last six months is really remarkable. He is quite fit to begin his studies for ordination now; and I should strongly advise them being undertaken as soon as possible. I have no idea how long his heart will hold out, for he is actually a very old man; so the less delay there is the better it will be for him."

The Abbot looked up rather abstractedly:

"Leave it over for a fortnight, Father. I must go to London on unexpected and urgent business. I am booked to give a retreat at the Convent in Seaham, but I cannot possibly put off the journey to London. I was just going to send for you, when you came in, to ask you to take my place at Seaham. You are the only suitable man available. I will wire at once to the Prioress about the change, and to the Bishop for your Faculties. So Brother Petroc must wait till we return. I do not like to launch out on any fresh experiment while we are both out of the house and there is no one to watch results. As you say, there is no great reserve of physical strength, and I promise you, on my return, I will at once make active preparations for him to receive just sufficient instruction for ordination."

"The Subprior went upstairs to Petroc's cell, and there he found his patient sitting on his favorite window-seat, smiling to himself.

"Father Abbot and I have to go away for a fortnight," he said.

Brother Petroc's face fell a little. He was very fond of the Abbot, but in the Subprior he had the unbounded confidence of a child for its father.

"But," continued he, "as soon as we get back, Father Abbot is going to consider the question of your preparation for the priesthood."

Brother Petroc smiled up at the Subprior, one radiant gleam of a smile; then he turned and whispered to the night:

"*Nunc dimittis servum tuum, Domine, secundum verbum tuum in pace.*"*

"Not yet, not yet awhile, Brother," said the Subprior, and he went quickly out.

---

* "Now you let your servant go in peace, Lord, according to your word."

Chapter Seven

The Prior of S. Brioc's was a most capable man. He dealt with the material affairs of the house in an eminently businesslike and effective fashion. An excellent Religious and a thoroughly conscientious Superior, he regarded the spiritual and temporal welfare of his monks as a matter for which he would be called to a most rigorous account. But he was a much occupied man, a little wanting in imagination perhaps, and for that reason a little wanting also in sympathy. He was kindly disposed to Brother Petroc, but had not much use for him, and was inclined to think the interest and attention shown him by the Abbot and Subprior somewhat excessive.

Dom Maurus was Guest Master, and had charge of the parish besides. He likewise was a most exemplary Religious, a great man of affairs, who considered himself a connoisseur in twentieth-century souls, with all their turnings and intricacies. It was part of a certain unconscious pose he had adopted, to profess a wide knowledge of and sympathy with all the ways by which souls are led to God. He considered that methods of self-examen were peculiarly suited to the introspective temper of the age; but he was apt to forget that no two souls are made to one pattern and that each must be led to perfection according to its individual temper and habits. Directly people begin to label souls and put them, so to speak, in pigeon-holes, the view of a great part of their varied beauty is lost. He was chaplain to the Convent of a modern Congregation which had charge of the school in the town. He professed great admiration for their life and often said he knew no better people, and his estimate of their sterling worth was certainly right.

For a day or two after the departure of the Abbot and Subprior, Brother Petroc was left in his wonted peaceful attitude. Life was made as easy as possible by the Brother Infirmarian, who was very kind to him, and his friends the Novices who were devoted to him. In himself too he was happy and at peace in a serene, affectionate detachment in regard to those round him, while the time he spent in the tribune for the sick grew longer. When a man's human interests and loves are separated from him by four hundred years, outward happenings do not make any very great odds. On the other hand the eternity of God makes Him always, as it were, a Contemporary.

But Petroc was not so unobserved as he thought himself, and he would have been more than a little surprised to learn that Dom Maurus was watching him with keen interest. Until the eve of the Abbot's departure, Dom Maurus, like the Prior, had had very little use for this strange, quiet man; besides, he was looked upon as, to a great extent, the property of the Subprior, and Dom Maurus was not one to meddle lightly in another's concerns. But Dom Maurus had been in the Abbot's room the evening before the latter went to London when the subject of Petroc's studies and ordination had been touched on, and he had learnt that, on the Superior's return, the dreamer—as he had designated Petroc in his own mind—was to begin, or rather revise, his studies for the priesthood. After this Dom Maurus began to study him with more attention, and the more he observed the more utterly he failed to see how in the world his ordination could be brought about. The man knew nothing and was in touch with nothing. In fact, unless some means of waking him to the practical realities of life could be devised, the Guest Master could see no chance of the priesthood for this unfortunate man who after all had waited four hundred years for ordination. And the pity of it was that the Abbot and Subprior, his friends, did not seem to realize the necessity of bringing him in touch with life. However, he, Dom Maurus, did realize this necessity and, if he could take a hand in the awakening, the poor brother would doubtless, and with good reason, bless him forever.

With the Guest Master decision and action were synonymous, so he went to the Prior's door and knocked.

"Father Prior," he said, "I have to go to one or two places in the town this afternoon and I thought of extending my walk along the cliffs. May I take Brother Petroc with me? A breath of fresh air and a little gentle exercise will do him good."

Now the Prior was busy reading, sorting, docketing and answering letters, so he half turned with the pen in his hand, said "Certainly" in preoccupied tones, made a note on the back of an answered letter and straightway forgot all about the request. The Guest Master was always coming in on small affairs connected with his office, and it was always safe to grant so reliable a man the permissions he sought without listening too closely to the exact tenor of all he said.

Dom Maurus next found the Brother Infirmarian—he intended to do all things in order—and told him that he had leave to take Brother Petroc for a walk.

"Don't go too fast, or too far, Father," said the Brother, "his heart is not at all strong and he can't do as much as the rest of us."

So Dom Maurus promised; they all made rather too much fuss over the supposed delicacy of a man who looked robust enough, but he would humor their foible. Finally he went to Brother Petroc's cell and told him the Prior wished him to accompany him for a walk. Petroc, always happy to be of service, came out at once and, as they wore their habits in the little town, the pair sallied forth without delay.

Dom Maurus, as we have said, knew very little about Petroc and he did not realize that the Brother had never faced the town and its traffic; he had only watched it from the cliff. Even the walk to Polgarth had been taken across country and the Novices had skirted the town. It never entered Petroc's head, either, to acquaint his companion with this fact; he simply took the obedience as it came.

At first all went well, for the Monastery lane was a very quiet place; then just as they came to the turning on to the high road, a motor car whizzed by and Petroc started back like a nervous horse. Before they had gone more than a hundred yards down the road, another went past in the opposite direction; it was followed by a motor bicycle with a side car; after this a lorry laden with ice lumbered down. Cold sweat broke out all over Petroc and nervous shivers ran down his spine. He glanced sideways at his companion who was holding on his way with a perfect sang-froid, so he gathered himself together and set his teeth.

The main road from Polgarth was one of the old thoroughfares, so it ran straight into the heart of the little town without touching the residential quarters, which extended on the side of the valley opposite the Abbey. The streets, in this part of the town, were old, steep and cobbled. Horses and carts, lorries, cars and wagons clattered up and down. A schooner was loading slate on the little quay at the far end, and the clank of windlasses and cranes and the shouts of men blew up the street. It happened moreover to be market afternoon and, according to custom, booths and stalls had been set up all down the street and in the square, which opened out on one side. The place was full of townsfolk and farmers from the surrounding countryside, who stood in groups round the stalls, bargaining and joking.

Petroc was in an agony. His ears were deafened by the jumble of noises; his unaccustomed eyes flickered with the kaleidoscope which shifted round him; a small one in reality, but to him colossal. A hammer seemed to be beating somewhere in his brain and he felt almost as if the movement and noise were within him instead of outside. If only everything would stop for just one little moment! He had however a sturdy will and plenty of self-control; besides, his companion was serenely making his way through the little crowd, totally unconscious of what the silent man at his side was enduring. So Petroc held on with set teeth.

At last there came a respite; turning up a side street flanked by a long blank wall, Dom Maurus made his way to a grated door, set in the masonry at the far end.

"The Convent of the 'Daughters of Fortitude,'" he said in bland explanation and rang the bell.

The Sister who opened the door took them straight into a little bare parlor and said she would fetch Reverend Mother.

"I am Chaplain here," Dom Maurus told Petroc when she had gone, "so they know me well. I have a message about the schools to give Reverend Mother. She is a very holy woman whom you will like to know."

Brother Petroc bowed.

When Dom Maurus had concluded his business with the Superior he half turned towards his companion:

"This Brother is a stranger, Reverend Mother, who knows very little about modern Religious Congregations and their life. Would you be so kind as to tell him a little?"

So the Superior in all simplicity began. She told him of their Meditation; five minutes for Preludes and Composition of Place, ten minutes for the first Point, ten for the second, and the last five for Resolutions and Spiritual Bouquet. She explained their method of Particular Examen with conscience book or beads; the hourly practice of the Presence of God; the pause for a sentence, from some spiritual book, twice during recreation; the time allotted for spiritual intercourse; the offering made at Mass, on their Rosary beads, directly after the Elevation; and very much more to the same purpose, while Brother Petroc sat listening with wide, bewildered eyes and damp hands clenched tight in his big sleeves. His mind, trained four hundred years ago, could neither grasp the essential difference between his own and many modern souls, nor understand the kind of discipline which was used by them. He only knew that he was up against the unknown and that the woman speaking to him was good above the ordinary.

"Two more visits and then we will discuss these questions, while we walk home along the cliffs," said Dom Maurus, as at last they emerged. And Brother Petroc bowed his assent, for his mouth was too stiff and dry to utter a word.

After walking for some minutes along the main road, they turned up a side one, which was bordered by typical seaside villas of pink stucco. They stopped before one, with a may tree on the front lawn and rustic palings. They walked up to a front door delicately painted in pale green, and Dom Maurus rang the bell.

"I have just come to enquire how Miss Jackson is after her journey to Rome," said he.

"Come in, Father; Miss Jackson is at home and will be delighted to see you," answered the trim maid, leading the way to a most aesthetic-looking drawing-room.

Miss Jackson was a "middle-aged" young lady, tall and thin. She had brushed her bobbed hair into a dank, Isabella-colored curtain round her head; her eyes were rather prominent, and she had cultivated a mental attitude of sweet expectancy, until her whole expression much resembled that of a highly intellectual codfish. Her green frock matched the paint on her front door. She was delighted to see Dom Maurus and spoke very beautifully and at length about her impressions of Rome; "not hard dry facts, Father, but the subtle effect on a mind attuned to receive such impressions." She spoke of spiritual odors and savors, touches and emotions, which, emanating from the soul, pervaded the very body. She touched on the subject of mystic experience, in a head voice very delicately modulated and with most careful attention to enunciation.

Brother Petroc was far beyond following much that she said for he was in a maze of bewilderment and misery. When at length Dom Maurus rose to go, his companion followed him hardly conscious of what he was doing.

"This is obviously a case of pseudo-mysticism run riot," remarked the Guest Master, and to himself he added: *"this poor young brother must be almost mental; he says nothing and apparently thinks nothing. However, I have done my best for him."*

The last visit, paid to a choleric old gentleman, in a high state of indignation at the "sinful increase of population among the poorer classes," made no separate impression at all, but merely added its quota to the crushing mass which was overwhelming Petroc.

Then, the three visits concluded, Dom Maurus, as he had promised, took him home over the cliffs. He was very kind and careful, walking slowly and helping his companion whenever they came to a hill, with a sustaining hand under his arm. As he walked, he discoursed.

Brother Petroc must, of course, realize the great difference between the modern mind and the mind as he had known it. People nowadays lived much more rapidly, their nerves were more sensitive, their tendency was more self-introspective. S. Benedict and the older Masters of the Spiritual Life had started with God and viewed the soul from that standpoint. Self-knowledge came through a comparison of their own souls with God, at Whom they were looking, and the desire that arose therefrom of rendering themselves as little unworthy of Him as possible. This was the view of S. Catherine of Siena, when Our Lord had told her: "I am He Who is, thou art she who art not." Now the later exponents started with the soul itself and cleansed and disciplined it systematically, in order to make it fit for the entrance of God. In many cases this point of view was peculiarly applicable to the self-introspective character of the modern mind. People's self-consciousness, if he might so put it, rendered this preliminary cleansing imperative before they could turn to God. Meditation, as understood by these later exponents, was an essential part of the system. The Particular Examen with its gradual lessening of one fault, by means of some tangible way of keeping a record of the efforts made, was another essential part. The tendency certainly seemed rather to over-emphasize the systematic side of Meditation, instead of regarding it merely as a stepping-stone to higher forms of prayer. But at any rate it served to prevent such deplorable misapprehensions as those from which Miss Jackson suffered. She had taken religion from a sentimental standpoint, which was neither wise nor wholesome. She had got hold of some notion of mysticism which was absolutely false; and the only redeeming feature seemed to be that she was such a foolish woman that no one would hold her responsible for her views. Of course, if she had a little more solidity a groundwork of systematic meditation would probably be the making of her. Reverend Mother, on the other hand, was an excellent example of the result of modern spirituality. Their own method of course was the older one and best suited to their Benedictine vocation; but it was as well for those, who would probably have the direction of souls, to see life from both these angles.

"And now, Brother, here we are at the Monastery gates again. I shall be very busy for the next few days. Later on however I hope to have other chances of taking you round and showing you things. We have only skimmed life, as it were, this afternoon. I would like you to see the poorer parts of the town, the life of the working people, their sufferings and temptations. But all in good time."

His victim shuddered involuntarily, but found voice nevertheless to thank him as they reached the door. Then turning quickly away he slipped up to his cell.

Chapter Eight

When Petroc returned, the Brother Infirmarian was too busy to pay much attention to him. Brother Placid, the gardener, had fallen over a tree-root and hurt his wrist so badly that they had sent for a doctor. The latter after examining the injury said that there was possibly a broken bone and that he would take the lay brother in his car to the Cottage Hospital at Polgarth for an X-ray examination. About ten minutes before Brother Petroc returned the doctor had driven his patient back, with the cheering news that there was nothing more serious amiss than a bad sprain. But what with the excitement and the bustle of putting Brother Placid, an old man and much shaken, to bed, the Infirmarian entirely forgot about Petroc and his walk. The latter however was far too stunned to pay much heed to anything. In a mechanical fashion he went to Vespers, Supper and Compline with the rest; but it was not until he had at last reached his cell and had seated himself on the window-seat that he began to think.

The Mountain of God, as he had known it, had been steep and rugged, but one climbed over the obstacles and journeyed straight on. Now, it seemed to him, people had made all sorts of paths by which to ascend the Mountain more easily, and none of these paths were familiar to Petroc. He realized as he had never done before how absolutely alone he was, for there was no living being whom he really understood and who understood him. People had never talked to him of spiritual things before, and now most of what he had heard that afternoon was simply Greek to him. The isolation he could bear, for he had had nearly a year of practice, but the worst trouble was that now God Himself was hidden somewhere in the distance and, Petroc thought, could only be reached by means of one of these bewildering paths.

He watched the moon rise and sink over the sea. He watched the tiny fishing fleet sail out and saw the dawning day. Then he came to a resolution, and crossing to the table sat down and rested his head on his folded arms and fell asleep. In an hour or so he awoke, and refreshed himself with a cold sponge; then he went down to Mass, bewildered still, but determined. Reverend Mother had said that Meditation led to God; Petroc had no doubt but that Reverend Mother herself was very close to God, so he set himself likewise to make a Meditation.

He went to the tribune of the sick and knelt down. Then he began to go through the process, as well as he could remember it, in his mind. First he must place himself in the Presence of God. But that he had already done by coming to make his prayer in the very House of God. There, below him, the Sanctuary lamp was glimmering an assurance that he was in the presence, the corporeal presence, of God the Son, the Second Person of the Blessed Trinity, made Man for us. Perhaps, in coming to Church, he had done all that was needful on this head. Next he remembered that he must make a Composition of Place. But why call his imagination to work when the reality was present? God Himself in the Tabernacle, and in his heart so close to him?

But was He there? Petroc was conscious of nothing but black darkness, in which there was no one but himself. It was no mere loss of sensible devotion, but a far worse blank. Human loneliness he could bear, but now his only friend, God, had left him. And he was utterly alone.

"My God!" he whispered, and bent his head on his hands.

There was a stir beside him presently. It was the Brother Infirmarian come to remind him that it was time for the Sung Mass. Brother Petroc had made no Meditation; not one Point! Obviously then Meditation was beyond his capacity, so that path was closed.

Later in the day he went back to the tribune to consider further his position and duties in regard to the Spiritual Life. For Brother Petroc was not one to be conquered at the first reverse. In the jumble of Dom Maurus' explanations, he remembered that something had been said about the essential necessity of Particular Examen.

Now this was not precisely what Dom Maurus had said; his discourse had been quite sound, though in view of the peculiar circumstances of his companion's life it had certainly been most unwise. For Lutheranism had not penetrated to Cornwall in Petroc's day; and so he had absolutely no knowledge of the needs to which S. Ignatius had ministered. Port Royal, the Jansenists and Quietism were still farther beyond any power of his to conceive. His spiritual vision was perfectly simple and straightforward; so that, in consequence, great patches of Dom Maurus' conversation had been absolutely unintelligible to him, and the little that had penetrated was quite out of its context. Moreover the life he was now living in a Benedictine Monastery, under the special care of the Abbot and Subprior, differed in no essential from that which he had lived in the same Monastery four hundred years ago. He had taken this identity as a matter of course, and had never thought of any difference being possible.

Now, in his pain and bewilderment, he began to wonder whether, under this life exteriorly so like his old one, an interior life of "modern spirituality"—the phrase was Dom Maurus'—was being lived by those around him. Petroc was very conscious of the fact that he had promised to try and live in the present. Perhaps living in the present meant also the adoption of "modern" forms of spirituality. In that case it was his obvious duty to attempt to follow these modern forms, and try to find his way along one or other of these paths which puzzled him so. He had proved to himself that he could not meditate;

perhaps he might do better with the Particular Examen. The first thing to do was to find his Predominant Passion. But which was the fault that lay at the root of all the rest? For the first time he deliberately reverted to that dream life of his, four hundred years ago; a life which was closed now. Facts and thoughts stood out in a series of sharp little vignettes. He saw a small boy in a white heat of anger over some childish vexation. He saw a young monk standing in his stall and trying not to wish that Sunday Matins were a little shorter. He remembered the half-stunned joy of his Profession day. But he could find no sequence; cause and effect would not connect. Well! As far as he could remember he had lived there looking towards God. There had of course been many faults of frailty, and sometimes there had been a certain deliberation in what he had done. Still, he fancied his face had been set right.

Now in regard to his present life—even here memory did not seem to serve him much better.

He thought he had tried to see God in these strange new Brethren of his, and to make his present life, an even stranger dream than the other, as far as he could, a solid reality. It had been hard at times, but—this predominant fault—my God! If the world were black and dreary, in which he was groping for the reality of God, his own soul was infinitely blacker and more dreary, and there was no God there either. He could not face—what was it?—self-introspection; the very word sounded cold and cruel. How his head ached! His mind too was clouded over. To make it work was just like turning the rusty key of the cellar when he was a Novice years and years ago.

It was useless. He could not meditate. He could not even find a starting-point for the Particular Examen. He was just an old man—an old, old man—a half-witted fool—four hundred years old. God! What an eternity!

He pulled himself together. This way certainly led nowhere. Yes it did; it led one way, it led to madness. If God Almighty asked that of

Petroc as well as the rest, His Will be done; but Petroc had no right to take one step of his own accord in that direction. So there remained only one course for him to pursue. He could make nothing of "modern spirituality." He must leave his soul and his spiritual life absolutely in the hands of the God Who was surely somewhere in the dark.

So hereafter Brother Petroc bowed to the inevitable and acquiesced in his own inability to cope with life, as men lived it now. God Almighty would save him somehow he supposed; Petroc would leave the issue to Him; and in the meantime there was nothing for it but to set his teeth and endure.

Chapter Nine

Brother Petroc's attitude of acquiescence in the inevitable did not last long, and it was Brother Leo who was the unconscious means of rousing his mind to active questioning. In many ways Brother Petroc's outlook was that of a man of the renaissance, though he had no share in the skepticism that the New Knowledge brought in its train.

On Thursday afternoon it was Brother Leo's turn to be instructor and, as the day was fine and warm, he proposed spending the lesson hour in the copse where Petroc had found the first daffodils. They walked down in silence, Brother Petroc lagging a little and walking with bent head and listless air. When they reached the copse, Brother Leo settled his friend comfortably against a fallen tree-stump, whilst he stretched himself luxuriously on the ground at his pupil's feet. The air was full of the fresh, tart smell of young growth, mingled with the subtle fragrance of the undergrowth of a shrubbery, while the copse rang with the song of birds.

Brother Leo sniffed appreciatively.

"What a heavenly smell!" he remarked.

Brother Petroc stiffened to attention. *Spiritual odors and savors, which emanating from the soul pervaded the very body*; the words flashed through his mind. The lad at his feet had just spoken of a heavenly smell. Perhaps Petroc had found the key to one puzzle.

"Is it only perceptible to the spiritually minded, Brother?" he enquired.

Brother Leo began to laugh; then glancing at his companion's face and finding it quite serious and a little anxious, he checked himself and answered.

"I'm afraid I don't quite understand."

"I gather from somewhat that I have heard that there are 'scents and savors' which emanate from a soul which has been touched by grace, and are perceptible to the bodily senses. Now I am totally ignorant of such matters. The relics of saints, other holy things and sometimes living saints give out at times sweet odors, I know. But as I understand the matter, the senses are the gates of knowledge and being affected by such things the mind is drawn to enquire the reason for such unearthly fragrance. Then the intellect, understanding the value of a holiness which is apparent even to the gross senses and being prevented and followed by grace, moves the will to a determination to follow the example of such sanctity. But how apprehension, which is a non-material faculty, can influence the senses of him who exercises the faculty in such a way as to cause them to perceive odors and savors which have emanated from this faculty, I cannot at all understand. Yet you who are a young man of sense spoke just now of a heavenly smell. Hence I must conclude that you are enjoying through your senses somewhat which has emanated from your non-material soul, since for my part I can perceive naught save the earthly fragrance of a fine spring day."

Brother Leo gasped a little, then pulling himself together answered very gently and humbly:

"I am sorry, Brother, to have misled you by a wrongly used word. I can smell no more than you, but I used the word heavenly in the sense of delightful. Surely your idea with regard to our senses and interior faculties is the correct one."

"Yet, Brother, on Monday I heard someone, who undoubtedly served God, speak of such things."

"People talk a lot of such nonsense nowadays. Instead of using their reason, they depend on imagination for their Spiritual life and it leads them badly astray."

"It is a strange world, Brother. People of this generation seem to place themselves in the centre of their universe and to look at life from that standpoint."

"It is an inevitable result of the trend of modern thought," said Brother Leo, becoming the complete scholastic, "and moreover the tendency to introspection is growing. There is a fascination in watching what goes on inside one. I count myself a good Benedictine enough, yet I find myself and my oddities quite an interesting object of study. This tendency shows itself everywhere. For instance psychoanalysis is a new and important factor in medicine. I don't know much about it, but I understand that nerves, neurasthenia and a host of kindred diseases are caused by some suppressed emotion. If this emotion and its cause can be found out and put right, the patient recovers. This leads to all sort of different methods of dealing with…juvenile crime, for instance. In the first stages a method called sublimation is used. A child has for instance a tendency to violent passion, thieving and such like. In most cases the first scientific attempt to cure it is by giving the child some legitimate exercise ground for the fundamental tendency at the back of the evil one shown; this is called sublimation. For example, a small thief is encouraged to make collections of stamps, post-cards and what not, and this turns his overgrown acquisitive tendency into a good and safe channel, thereby removing the cause which led to his thieving. We are all concerned with human nature in itself and by itself these days."

Brother Petroc sat staring with unseeing eyes at a busy nest-building thrush. After a minute or two he said slowly:

"We would have chastised such children when they were young, and as they grew older would have shown them that such acts were an offence against God. Truly life in this twentieth century is very much changed. Men seem to think that it is the spiritual faculties which affect the senses. Now we considered that the contrary was true. A man suffering from accedia was set to dig or other manual labor, until he was wearied out and the brother body left the soul in peace. We were taught to guard our senses as the gateways of the soul, and when those senses became too importunate we tamed them by penance. After that the spiritual man was safe enough. My soul was never nearer God than when I took my turn in bakehouse or garden, but my body and my senses were not aware of this nearness, for I wearied them by hard work and then bade them be silent while my soul communed with God. But alas! I have lost Him now in the dark; and mayhap He means me to seek Him as you do. I fear I am too old to learn new ways, but I will endeavor."

"I think you are off the track there, Brother; after all we are all Benedictines and must live as Our Holy Father taught us. Any difference in outlook is a mere accident caused by our living in different centuries."

"Mayhap, mayhap! But it seems I ought to bridge the gap made by the passing of time, since God willeth me to live now, in this twentieth century. Answer me this question, if you will, Brother; when you set yourself to prayer, what do you do?"

"I first place myself in the Presence of God."

"You go to the Choir? But that is natural, is it not?"

"I didn't quite mean that. I recollect myself, recalling to my mind Him to Whom I am about to speak, so that I may approach Him with due reverence."

"That also is necessary. For Ecclesiasticus saith: 'Before prayer, prepare the soul and be not as a man that tempteth God.' But 'tis strange to name so simple an act. What do you next?"

"I take some verse of the Psalms, or other passage of Holy Scripture, and use it as a starting point, giving me, as you might say, a beginning for my conversation with Almighty God."

"That also I understand. But not long since I heard a very good woman speak of Preludes and Points and a Spiritual Bouquet. What of these, Brother?"

"I am afraid I don't know very much about such things. I was educated at Downside. You must get hold of some Jesuit book if you want to study that form of Mental Prayer. Still, if you don't mind my saying so, I would not bother much about such things. They don't affect our life as Benedictines and you surely have enough necessary study without worrying yourself with non-essentials. But do you know, Brother Petroc, we shall have to hurry back? Our hour is up, and I shall be catching it from Father Master if I am late for class."

They made the best of their way to the Monastery, and Brother Petroc went up to his cell somewhat soothed and comforted despite the ever present sense of loneliness and desolation. All might therefore have ended well if an evil fate had not sent Father Prior to Petroc's cell that afternoon in order to leave him a letter from the Subprior. Now the editor of one of the Catholic papers had sent Father Prior a little book to review. It was a small volume in a sky-blue cover entitled *The Beaten Track to God*, and was written by a certain F.D., obviously a woman. Father Prior had skimmed the book, had written a slashing criticism and was conveying the sky-blue volume to oblivion in the lumber room, when he stopped on his way at Petroc's cell with the letter. On coming into the room his eye caught a broken window-cord. He laid down the book and letter in an absent-minded fashion on the table and walked across the room to examine the damage. Then he went out without again remembering the book. Brother Petroc coming in not long after discovered both book and letter, and naturally concluded that someone who guessed his trouble had left him a remedy. He knew nothing about an Imprimatur, so the blank sheet facing the title-page gave him no warning.

It really was a dreadful little book, but in the two hours that Petroc had free before Vespers, he read it from cover to cover, obtaining therefrom much astounding information, interspersed with anecdotes.

Among other things, he learnt that the human soul was a mass of corruption which required very drastic treatment. F.D. gave a minute regimen, which was to be carefully followed if cure was desired. A thorough sifting of sins, motives, temptations and possible temptations was to occupy ten minutes twice daily. Then there was to be an hour's Meditation made every morning according to a most careful prescription. The exact nature of, and time to be given to, each preliminary, the time given to each point and what acts were to be made, everything was scheduled like a railway time-table. The conclusion likewise was dealt with in great detail and was carried out in close connection with the two daily soul excoriations. The rest of the day was mapped out in periods of a given length, and each was begun by a particular pious exercise which was to color the whole period. An appendix gave an edifying list of prayer books and beads of all kinds and where they were obtainable. If all the devotional objects there mentioned were to be efficiently dealt with, the permanent companionship of a good-sized attaché case would be necessary.

F.D. described in another chapter the terrible pitfalls which lie in wait for the unwary. One of the most insidious of these was named Contemplation, or Mysticism, which was described as a gift granted to Saints alone and not to be desired or sought by those who wished to escape spiritual pride. Apparently, Petroc discovered, this was responsible for the strange odors and savors, voice and visions he found so unpalatable. Meditation was the all-important means of avoiding this terrible snare; Meditation according to F.D.'s exposition. Any attempt to escape from the scheduled time-table and to catch, so to speak, an express, was fatal and inevitably led down to…Contemplation.

The anecdotes were every bit as surprising. One gentleman had attained great heights of sanctity by the assiduous following of the Fourth Addition of S. Ignatius; what that Addition might be F.D. did not care to specify. Another, a woman this time, had eliminated all traces of sin in a very short space of time by means of arithmetical calculations on a string of beads.

F.D. showed great tact throughout in careful suppression of the essential of her tales: the zeal and love of God, which had led these people to adopt whatever means presented itself to them, by which they could reach Him; and F.D. laid an equally careful stress on details which were simply the individual soul's means of correcting faults and attaining the end.

It is very doubtful whether this little book under ordinary circumstances would have caused Brother Petroc any more than mild amusement. But his experiences of Monday afternoon had rendered him, for the time, super-sensitive and anxious. Besides he thought that the book had been left for his special benefit; and the result was a night of anguish.

In the old days his Master had taught him that he belonged to a Contemplative Order, and that watchful attention to God would most probably result in the gift of Contemplation. This was certainly to be petitioned for and desired; but he was taught to distinguish between the gift of prayer and those phenomena, often the result of weakness of soul, which sometimes accompanied it and were neither to be sought nor desired. In his days, silent prayer and the recitation of the Divine Office had been part of one whole, each strengthening the other. There were no divisions and subdivisions such as were made later.

He felt there must be something very wrong in him to make him so critical of a book which had obviously been left for his instruction. Yet when Brother Leo had spoken of prayer that afternoon he had used a tongue familiar to Petroc;

and, in Petroc's own estimation, the soul of the young man was certainly in that watching, receptive state most apt for God's gift. It was very puzzling.

Petroc likewise had learnt to examine his conscience. He had been taught to offer a rapid prayer for light, to take one rapid glance over the day, certain that any deliberate fault would stand out, to make an equally rapid survey of the time to come with probable temptations. This was followed by a short, loving Act of Contrition for sins past, and a swift prayer for help and guidance in the future. There he had learnt to make a leisurely, detailed Act of Thanksgiving for all the graces, joys and sorrows of the day just gone. He must own himself a fool, but he doubted his ability to spend much time in microscopic examination of his soul and its poor frailties.

At last the trained intellect and the alert, eager mind asserted themselves. Was it necessary, or even right, to take all this strange new spirituality on faith as better than his own? Let him test even one chapter of the sky-blue book by certain acid tests he had learnt.

Accordingly next morning he reduced the first chapters of the *"Vade Mecum"* as far as he could to logical form; then he took the analysis, with its resulting syllogisms, to pieces bit by bit, and examined it. His examination led to an unhesitating rejection of the contents of the little volume with a prayer that spiritual pride might not lead him astray. He left the papers of syllogistic argument and refutation just inside the book and went down to his work.

That afternoon, for the first time, Brother Gregory, the Instructor for the day, found his pupil somewhat critical and even a little irritable. Among other things he happened to refer to his Novice Master as an "awfully kind man," and received in return a sharp rebuke for ambiguity of terms. "Kindness," said his pupil, "was not an awe-inspiring virtue."

Later on he found himself floundering badly in a perfect quagmire of self-contradiction, and instead of the helping hand usually extended at such times he was left to extricate himself as best he could, unaided. At the end of the lesson the pupil apologized very humbly to his heated, flustered master; he was very sorry but somehow patience had been wanting to him today, and in any case he considered that he had been entirely lacking in ordinary courtesy.

Chapter Ten

The next morning, as the Prior was making a final revision of his critique, it suddenly flashed into his mind that he had left the obnoxious blue book together with the Subprior's letter in Petroc's cell on the previous afternoon. Now even the prior realized that *The Beaten Track* was hardly a suitable book for a pre-Reformation monk, so he hurried upstairs, somewhat perturbed, to retrieve it.

Petroc was in the Sacristy but had left the book on his table. It was lying just where the Prior had left it, and for one brief moment the latter hoped that it had been undiscovered. As he carried it downstairs, however, he noticed quite a wad of paper covered with Petroc's careful script, tucked just inside the front cover.

When he reached his room he opened the book and took out the manuscript, intending to return it, but stood transfixed when he realized that it was a logical analysis of F.D.'s opening chapters written in careful Latin.

Fascinated and entertained, he followed Petroc's refutation of the arguments. There were pages like the following:

"*Argument to prove the necessity of much self-introspection.*—All corruption and disease are things which require frequent attention and much handling.

> The human soul is a mass of disease and corruption.
> Therefore the human soul requires frequent attention and much handling.
> Valid Syllogism in Barbara.
> But I deny the Minor Premise for:

> All things made by God are beautiful.
>
> The human soul is made by God.
>
> The human soul is beautiful.
>
> Further, though it be touched by original sin and its consequences, which the soul inherits,
>
>> Original sin is an inherited mark or stain,
>>
>> But a mark or stain does not necessarily mean disease and corruption.
>
> But granted that Mortal sin is disease and corruption the Major Premise is a *Petitio Principii* for no proof is given that disease and corruption require much handling. Practical experience proves that such handling spreads the evil and experiment proves that cauterization is the best method of dealing with corruption. Hence a soul is best cleansed in the Furnace of Divine Love."

In connection with F.D.'s minute round of pious practices, the Prior found:

> "Each of these devotional acts in itself is good, Therefore all taken together will be better still.
>
> A Priori Argument containing the Fallacy of Composition.
>
> By analogy with this it might be argued
>
> > Bread is good, meat is good, milk, eggs, fish, etc. are all good.
> >
> > Hence when all are taken at once they are still better."

The Prior read every word to the bitter end: but when he reached the last sheet and turned over the page, he found the logician in a new guise. For Petroc had been using scraps of paper, and on the back of one he had already written a lyric. The Brother laid no claim to being a poet, but he was undoubtedly an artist; an unexpectedly mild morning in February, when the hoar frost had turned to diamonds and the sun shone through an iridescent mist, had prompted the artist in him to express itself in the nearest medium at hand. This is what the Prior read:

Iam Hiems Transiit

Of winter-thorn and white-thorn
Fain would I sing,
Of Marye Flower of Heaven,
Of Chryste our King.

It fell about the Yule-tide,
When winds are starke and wilde,
That of a mayden stainless
Was born a littyl Childe.

It fell about the Spring-time,
When flowers are fresshe to see,
That Chryste, the Sonne of Marye
Did die uponne a tree.

When alle was dead in winter
A new-born Baby cryed.
When every tree was quick with bud
The Sonne of Marye died.

Of winter-thorn, of winter-thorn
I sing straynge lullabye,
In Chryste the dead are quickened
In Chryste for love wee dye.

Of white-thorn, fayre white thorn,
Of Chryste's crowne I sing,
Of Marye, Flower of Heaven
Of Chryste our Joye and Kyng.

The Prior walked over to the window and stood staring out at the lawn with its border of rough-hewn granite blocks, the path covered with a gravel of granite chippings that sparkled in the sun, and the wrought iron gate flanked by pillars on which two grinning bears rampant, in granite, bade defiance to any unauthorized person who should venture within the enclosure. Petroc had seen those bears, less weather worn perhaps, keeping guard on his Monastery four hundred years ago, and now he came to his own place almost as a guest of the stranger monks, his Brothers nevertheless, who stood in the stalls occupied by himself and his contemporaries in the days of the Sixth Edward.

He was a strange man certainly, the product of another era, with a very different outlook. The Prior's own ideas about Petroc certainly required readjustment. He was not the half-witted dreamer that the Prior had thought him. He had a keen well-trained mind, a sane, well-balanced judgment and a real sense of humor. Added to that he was a poet too and the juxtaposition of poetic talent and relentless logic was none too common nowadays. The Prior hardly remembered that this juxtaposition was characteristic of Petroc's own day. Well! thank goodness Petroc had appreciated *The Beaten Track* at its proper worth and the Subprior, on his return, would not be raging like a lion round the house to discover who it was who had given his patient scruples.

Furthermore, use could and ought to be made of him. In the first place, the summer visitors were just beginning to arrive at S. Brioc, and as a matter of course paid a visit to the picturesque old Monastery on the cliff. Who was more fitted than Petroc to show them round the Church and give the history of the building? After all he knew the place as no one else did, and these papers of his showed his ability to cope with the strangers and their questions.

Now this was all very well as far as it went; but the Prior forgot to take into account the fact that life was still so bewildering and strange to Petroc that to lay a task of this kind on him was to add a heavy strain.

As the Prior stood laying his plans, he saw a telegraph boy making his way past the bears and up the path to the door. He brought a wire from the Abbot saying that he had been obliged to send for the Subprior and stay another fortnight in

London and telling the Prior to send Dom Maurus to give a ten days' retreat at the Cenacle in Polgerran. This fitted in quite conveniently with the arrangements that the Prior was already contemplating, for now he would tell the Sacristan to act as temporary Guest Master and put Petroc in his place. So he sent for Dom Maurus and, having given him his orders, went in search of Petroc.

The latter was in his cell busy with a letter to the Subprior. He rose on his superior's entrance with a rather harassed, haunted air. What was coming next? He felt as if life had taken the bit in its teeth and run away with him.

"I left a small book here by accident, Brother, when I left your letter yesterday afternoon," said the Prior. "I am glad that you seemed perfectly capable of estimating it at its proper worth."

Brother Petroc went crimson and suppressed a tiny sigh.

"By accident, Father Prior? That is good. I feared the book contained some new form of spirituality which I needs must learn."

"And yet you examined it piecemeal?"

Petroc hesitated a moment at the new word. "Piecemeal?" he queried.

"In detail, Brother, argument by argument."

"At first, Father Prior, I was much distressed, for I thought that the book was placed there for my instruction; and it seemed to me very strange. Then I bethought me that I had a God-given wit of my own and moreover, in my early days, had been taught to use it. So I examined the treatise as we should have done years ago and found its reasoning, in my estimation, greatly to seek. So I decided, albeit in much anxiety of mind, to reject its teaching."

"I am glad, Brother, that you showed so much good sense and discrimination. I should have been more than sorry if through my carelessness the book had upset you. But I have a piece of news for you. I have heard from Father

Abbot that he and Father Subprior find it necessary to be away for another fortnight. I have also had instructions to send Father Maurus to Polgerran to give a retreat there, so we shall be very shorthanded. Under the circumstances then, until the Abbot comes back, I am going to ask you to take charge of the Sacristy, showing the visitors round the Church and explaining the place to them. It is a thing that you will be thoroughly competent to do. That will free the present Sacristan to act as temporary Guest Master, a job that I think you might find a little difficult."

Brother Petroc signed his assent, showing little of the inward perturbation he felt at the prospect before him. In his young days a good monk had obeyed any order given without question.

As soon as the Prior left him, he hurriedly finished his letter and went to the Sacristan to obtain detailed instructions as to his new occupation.

Chapter Eleven

Petroc soon found that his new occupation filled his time very completely. There were the Altars to be dealt with, vestments to be taken out and put away and the work of the Lay Brother to superintend. He obtained a list of his duties from the monk he superseded and was told to seek him in any difficulty which might arise. As many things were different from what Petroc had been accustomed to, he had to seek counsel pretty frequently.

Then there were three or four parties of visitors to be shown round the Church each day.

Petroc honestly loathed this part of his work. Most of the people grated on him; he did not understand them and they certainly did not understand him.

It was not long before they began to group themselves into several distinct categories. It somehow became easier for him after he had made them, so to speak, different parts of a system. He had some general notion, then of how to deal with them.

First there were those he designated the Jackson species. These people always began with a gushing series of remarks about the wonderful old Church, its links with the past and what it could tell them if it were endowed with speech. Then sooner or later one or the other of them was sure to sniff and then ask the others, in rather breathless tones, whether they did not perceive some unusual fragrance lingering about the place. On this the rest would raise their heads, just like a herd of does when the stag has winded some suspicious scent. Finally, they would all ask Petroc whether others had noticed it, and what it all meant.

Petroc found patience and charity severely tried at this stage of the proceedings. He generally answered somewhat abruptly that he knew nothing about any unusual scent, that the monks used a particularly good brand of incense which they obtained from abroad. There was also the Lady Altar paneled with cedarwood, the gift of a rich benefactor—probably that was what they smelt. He told one obnoxious lady that it was the scent she herself used; and afterwards accused himself to the Prior of impatience and pride.

There was another class who wished to obtain an extensive knowledge of the interior life of the monks and Petroc's own spiritual views. With these people he found the only safeguard was to confine himself strictly to monosyllables.

Then there were the heretics and schismatics. At first these caused Petroc considerable distress; later he excused them as soon as he realized that they meant no discourtesy to the Master of the

House when they entered without any outward sign of respect and walked about talking quite loudly.

They asked many questions, and some of these questions the monk found quite difficult to answer, for he himself knew next to nothing of their various beliefs or lack of belief. Some considered themselves, he discovered, an English branch of the Roman Church; these believed much of what Petroc believed. There were others, on the contrary, who did not even believe in the Divinity of Jesus Christ. Still others did not appear to believe in anything at all. Some took a sympathetic attitude with regard to the monk and his vocation; others startled him by questions of a distinctly unexpected kind. One lady asked him to tell her about the punishments and tortures in force in the monastery and obviously doubted him when he laughed and answered that he knew naught of such things. Another visitor opined that he had carried a broken heart into this shelter.

"Truly," answered Petroc, "it must have been early broken, since I was but nine years of age when I first came here."

One day an earnest gentleman took him on one side to beg him to fly the wiles of the Scarlet Woman, for he was worthy of the pure faith. He seemed rather surprised himself when Petroc naïvely enquired who she was and where she might be found. The monk was not much enlightened when he was told that she was "the whore who sat on the Seven Hills of Rome."

"Then the poor lost soul cannot have much influence over me here in Cornwall," answered Petroc, "and 'twould be sheer foolishness to fly a place in which she is not to be found, to risk meeting her by chance in the great wicked world."

And he turned away to show the rest of the party some other object of interest, leaving his would-be adviser nonplussed.

Then there came to the old Church historians, geologists, archaeologists and a host more. Petroc liked these well enough, for they were interested in matters which also interested him and they could fill gaps in his own knowledge.

Finally, there were those whom Petroc, in his mind, designated "Friends of God." These people slipped quietly into the Church and knelt, often just inside the door, to pay a visit to the Master of the House. Sometimes they walked quietly and reverently round the Church afterwards, sometimes they did not. In any case they seldom required his services and he was grateful to them.

Of course Petroc himself was hardly a figure to pass unnoticed. The spare, small, supple young monk, with a rather unusual carriage and movement, a half-unearthly face with brilliant, keen eyes, set mouth and slight air of aloofness, excited no little comment. If people came to see the Church, they also came during that fortnight to see Petroc, to listen to his half-foreign speech unlike anything they had ever heard before, to enjoy his unusual explanations and comments and to be piqued by some hidden mystery which made him, both in his knowledge and his ignorance, so unlike the rest of the world.

The Jackson species found him deliciously medieval, but somewhat lacking in a finer perception of things spiritual. The heretics were frankly puzzled; they had never met his like before. The savants found him a man of no little acumen and great reasoning power, coupled with the most extraordinary patches of blank ignorance. To the "Friends of God" he was one of the beautiful things of the Master's House.

The Prior, as we have said before, had not much imagination; moreover the monks by now were more or less used to Petroc; so he did not in the least realize the interest and curiosity which the Brother's speech and appearance were rousing among the summer visitors; otherwise he would have been the first to relieve the temporary Sacristan of his uncongenial task.

To Petroc himself the fortnight seemed endless. Each night he came to his cell worn out, not so much in body as in spirit. Each day was filled with a long succession of puzzles which he dare not try to solve. They were too many and too strange. For the sake of mind and soul he held curiosity firmly in leash, turned his mind away as quickly as might be from his new acquaintances and their ways, and asked no questions. It would have been easier if his own soul had not been so oppressed with desolation. It was hard to keep his mastery of self, and hold imagination and fear in check, when there seemed no God at hand to fill the empty house. He did his best; prayed, suffered and was silent.

The Novices found him rather lacking in interest and distinctly irritable at times. He was always very penitent afterwards, but it was unlike him to snap them up as he was doing now and they found their lessons by no means easy to give.

They referred the matter to the Novice master, who had been making observations on his own account.

"Be gentle and patient," he told them, "Brother Petroc is under a strain that no one realizes and his only two sympathetic friends are away. When Father Abbot and the Subprior come back they will take your pupil out of the Sacristy and guard him from outside contact, which is a great source of trouble to him. Father Prior is very good, but he does not understand him as they do, or he would never have asked him to undertake this office. Just pray for him and make the lesson hour as easy and amusing as possible."

To himself he added: "Thank God the Abbot will be back in a few days, otherwise I should certainly speak to the Prior to prevent a nervous breakdown. I think, as it is, he can hold on until they come back."

One evening, as Petroc was making preparations for the numerous Masses next day, the temporary Guest Master came into the Sacristy.

"You had better come over to the Guest House," he said. "We have a young Dominican spending the night here, on his way home from a Sanatorium down west, and you had better find out what he will do about Mass in the morning; I suppose he will follow the Benedictine Kalendar in this Church, but just come over and see."

As soon as he was free Petroc made his way over to the large room on the first floor generally reserved for priest guests. A cheerful voice answered his knock and he opened the door to find a very tall, very thin young man, in a white habit, busily engaged in making a bed up on the sofa under the open window.

"Good evening, Brother," said the young man cordially. "I am afraid you will think my occupation very unusual; pulling a comfortable bed to pieces in this way. But it struck me as a very poor return for your hospitality to scatter germs round your room, therefore I am making a bed right under the window so as to encourage as many as possible to try sea breezes by night. Besides, they tell me the disease is quiescent just now so that should make things safe for you all."

"You are ill then, Father?" queried Petroc, somewhat taken by this cheerful young man in the white habit, but shocked at his excessive thinness.

"I have been six months in a Sanatorium, near Land's End. But the doctors have decided that both my lungs have gone past repair. So our Provincial is allowing me to come home again. And I am returning to Woodchester with a sheaf of instructions on the best way to avoid giving my trouble to anyone else; hut in the garden, you know, and all that. But I really don't care now I'm going home again."

Petroc looked at his companion and smiled a little.

"So you will be going to God, shortly?" he asked.

The young man smiled back.

"They tell me six months will be the end of it. The last act in a glorious adventure. In a way, I am sorry not to have done more but there it is; and I have at any rate lived every moment of it."

He turned and looked out of the window.

"I am rather glad I can't see anything but the sea from here. Those dreadful outlying bungalows make one feel positively ill. I am not sure I don't prefer a downright town."

"Now I," said Petroc, "have not seen a downright town larger than Polgarth in my life."

"You are fortunate then. A big town is a blot on the face of God's earth. I was brought up in the country, but ever since taking my Lectorship five years ago I have lived nowhere but in towns. That's the way of it. You Benedictines live in your Monasteries in the country and say 'Come out here, like us.' We go into the big towns, so that we can say to the people: 'Get out of here as quickly as possible.' But the worst of it is that most of them won't listen. They prefer their hovels up a back street with a pub at hand and a cinema two or three streets away and the corner of their own back lane where they can stand in the mud with their backs against any convenient wall and their hands in their pockets, when work is slack."

Petroc stared.

"All this is beyond my ken," he answered; "how can men live so? And how can you endure to see it?"

The Dominican raised his eyebrows.

"Your experience and outlook are somewhat unusual, Brother," he said. "I suppose we none of us like it. But we Dogs of the Lord must be prepared to go down rabbit-holes if necessary."

"And of your spiritual life?" Petroc had fairly got to business now.

"Why much the same as yours. We are early thirteenth century, you know, and that is our best asset. You can say to these town dwellers 'Go away from here' with a clear conscience, when you are doing your best to let the Breath of God's Holy Spirit blow right through your own soul. To my mind, that's easiest done by Monastic discipline, though opinions differ. I suppose though that my work of that kind is over, and I must be content with using my pen as long as my strength holds out. What time do you sing Compline? I'll be singing it at home tomorrow, and I may as well get a foretaste of it in your Church tonight. It is six blessed months since I heard the *In manus tuas* and I can tell you I fairly ached to hear it sung by the most raucous novice who ever got on my nerves."

"We sing Compline at eight o'clock. And what about your Mass tomorrow?"

"Any time that will suit; I generally get all my coughing over pretty early in the night, thank goodness. And look here, Brother"—the young man was eyeing him in a wistful coaxing way—"I know I ought to say your Mass here; but I have one of my own Missals with me; they allowed me to go to the Church near the Sanatorium sometimes. Do you think Father Prior will let me say my own Mass? Tell him I shan't be able to do it much longer."

Petroc gave a ready promise to obtain the required permission, and left the room quite heartened. It seemed in a way as if he had met an old friend; and yet, he thought as he went downstairs, suppose he had come to life again in a

Dominican Priory, he would probably have found differences as strongly accentuated as likenesses.

Chapter Twelve

It was Friday, and Dom Maurus was due to return that afternoon, so to Petroc's inexpressible relief this season of contact with the strange modern world would come to an end that night. Moreover, he had heard from the Subprior that the latter was returning on the following Monday, while the Abbot would come back on Tuesday, so it appeared as if life would resume its normal round very shortly.

But on that Friday, Petroc had two unusual and unexpected visitors. In the morning he made acquaintance with a real Jesuit, and in the early afternoon he saw, for the last time, the mysterious woman over whom he had exercised such an involuntary influence.

His meeting with the Jesuit was in this wise. Petroc was filling the Holy Water stoups, when he saw a priest standing at the bottom of the Church intent on an old monument. It was the tomb of a Crusader, Sir Tancred Lanhednick, who had founded the Monastery and built the Church. The priest looked up as Petroc came near, and smiled. He was iron-grey, alert and ruddy, with keen, narrow eyes wrinkled at the corners and a soldierly carriage.

"Can you tell me how this Crusader in early thirteenth-century armor is carrying a late fourteenth-century shield?" he enquired.

Petroc's eyes twinkled; he had vivid recollection of what had happened over that shield.

"The effigy, some time about 1540, was injured by a falling beam, and we—they entrusted its repair to a monk who was better sculptor than historian," he answered. "There were other injuries done at the same time and the roof needed instant attention, so the monk was left alone to mend the effigy. When all was done he brought his Abbot to see the tomb. Father Abbot saw at once that the Brother had given Sir Tancred a shield he could never have borne; but he said that, since the rest was well done, the shield must remain as it was in memory of the ignorance of Brother Martin, and to serve him as a buckler against the dart of vain-glory."

"This is an exceedingly interesting Church you have here, Father, and as I happen to be something of an historian myself I should be greatly obliged if you could spare the time to take me round and explain things."

"You are a priest, as I see by your collar, sir. I am only a deacon as yet."

"Yes, Brother, a priest and moreover a Jesuit," said the newcomer, his eyes twinkling.

Brother Petroc sprung to attention; here was the chance of a little first-hand information about some at least of his puzzles. For had not Brother Leo suggested his learning in Jesuit books particulars as to Meditation and Examen?

"I have never spoken to a Jesuit before, and I know nothing about them. If I give you of my best concerning the Church and its history, perhaps you on your side would answer me a few questions."

The Jesuit's eyebrows rose a trifle. Perhaps a country yokel living in an out-of-the-way village in Cornwall might go through life ignorant of the Society of Jesus, but Petroc was evidently no yokel. Moreover his speech, though certainly different from modern English, was not the Cornish of some unlettered fisher lad. However, Petroc and his peculiarities were none of his business and one courtesy merited another, so he smiled and answered:

"By all means, Brother, I will answer your questions if I can."

The pair then proceeded to study the Church systematically and Petroc found his new acquaintance so well-read and interesting that he proposed obtaining the Prior's leave to take the Jesuit through other parts of the Monastery and grounds not generally shown to visitors.

"That is very kind of you, Brother. Perhaps you would like to take my card to the Prior," said the stranger.

The Prior gave a willing permission to extend the tour and when he saw on the card the name of a man well known throughout scientific circles for his brilliant research work he told Petroc further to take the visitor to the Guest House for lunch.

When the monk had exhausted his store of information and shown his guest everything worth seeing, he led him to a wall of rough-hewn granite overlooking the sea; and, after making his companion comfortable on a garden seat, opened fired.

Why were many of the modern forms of spirituality so different from the old? How were the Jesuits pioneers of one particular and very distinctive form? Why also was there another tendency which seemed a travesty of the older form run riot?

The Jesuit gave one keen glance at the amazing young man at his side and then said:

"May I smoke, Brother? I find it helps me to think and I should like to answer your questions as clearly as I can. The Company of Jesus was founded just when the Reformation was bringing an entirely new and very strong force to bear against the Church. This of course necessitated an equally new and strong counter attack on her side. If you will think for a moment, the era of which we are speaking was one of innovations; among other things a very different system was making its way into ordinary warfare. Single combats and knights with their men-at-arms, each carrying his food soldier with him on his horse, were giving place to trained bands of soldiers working, so to speak, in team fashion.

"The quality required in the new soldier was not any great personal bravery or prowess, but the capability of suppressing himself so as to work with the rest as part of one whole. Now the Church uses the weapons of the children of darkness when such serves her purpose, so she began to carry exactly the same principle into spiritual affairs. S. Ignatius, a soldier, had probably been interested in the changed war tactics, and by God's inspiration founded a spiritual army on exactly the same plan. The discipline necessary to form these new soldiers of Christ was supplied by the Spiritual Exercises, which fought the Reformers on their own ground. And in order to bring mind and will into the disposition which would enable his soldiers to act as parts of one whole instead of as individuals, the founder freed them from ordinary monastic discipline, such as the public recitation of the Divine Office, extra fasts and abstinence and so on. For these disciplined the body to let the souls go free, while S. Ignatius found it necessary to ease the body that it might be strong enough to bear his rigid discipline of mind and will.

"Naturally the perfection of individuals has suffered; for instance I should probably be a better specimen of an intellectual man if I were not a Jesuit. But to be a Jesuit is my vocation and in being true to it I am bound to subordinate my own advancement to the good of the Company as a body. With you older Orders the case is quite different; you are spiritual knights and the good of your body, as a whole, depends on your individual perfection and development.

"I think that answers your first and second questions; very briefly and sketchily I am afraid, but it will, I think, give you a glimpse of my idea. Now for the third. You realize, of course the position that systematization holds in development?"

"Yes, it is the final stage when enquiry is almost ended."

"Well! This present generation has a craze for systematizing everything it can lay hands on. Now premature systematization, as you know, means death to the further development of any living thing, since systematization implies maturity. The result of this craze is the death, in the individual, of all real spirituality, as people in their haste to reduce everything to system mistake the means for the end. They seize on outward manifestations and methods of spirituality and call that spirituality itself. Broadly speaking, the end of every kind of spiritual life is the same; Union with God by Charity. But since different people are called to different forms of service, their preparation and training and the means they use must necessarily be different and adapted to the form of service required of them. People see certain results in others, admire them, and immediately conclude the result is the infallible effect of the means used. In other words, they believe that a certain type of meditation must produce a certain type of holiness. This of course is rubbish, for the result is really obtained by the good-will and zeal with which any means are used.

"Then there are other people who object to these fanatics, who take the Jesuit way and use it as a kind of charm which will infallibly produce sanctity. S. Ignatius himself would certainly have been the first objector. But these other people are just as anxious to systematize as the first, though for them the pendulum is at the opposite end of the swing. For they reduce the older forms of spirituality to a series of formulae, again taking some quite accidental manifestation for the essence of the thing, and as a result they find themselves in even worse morasses of foolishness than the people whom they criticize. *The Imitation of Christ* says a good many hard things about such people.

"The real facts of the matter are that God has an individual call for every soul and clearly indicates the means by which that soul is to carry out His Will. But no one has any right to take to himself God's indication to another. It is where people attempt to follow others slavishly that the trouble begins. And that I think, Brother answers your questions to the best of my power."

"It is all true, quite true. If people were less the centre of their own universe much trouble and pain would be saved. But I read somewhere of a soul attaining sanctity by adhering to the Additions of S. Ignatius. What may these be?"

"When S. Ignatius organized his Company, he naturally gave them, so to speak, the Drill Book and Army Regulations they were to follow. Some good Jesuit, trying to live up to his vocation, kept a notebook to help him, in which he used a kind of code to remind himself of the virtues specially necessary for him. Someone, more zealous than discreet, publishes these private notes and immediately the world discovers that he is giving it a new magic formula for attaining sanctity. The same thing is observable all along, accidentals are confused with essentials."

"Things do not really appear"—Petroc pulled himself up short on the verge of a remark which might have betrayed him—he must not talk to this stranger about things as they had been in his day. So he smiled and added: "But you must be hungry, and the Guest Master will not be pleased with me if I spoil your meal by keeping you overlong."

And he led the Jesuit, interested and a little puzzled, back to the house.

In the early afternoon Petroc was again in the Church, trying to make up for his interrupted morning, when he saw kneeling at the bottom of the Church the girl who had accosted him earlier in the year. He had prayed for her with great perseverance, but he most emphatically did not want to meet her again. So he made a bee-line for the Sacristy.

He was putting out the Cope for Vespers when a sound made him look up. There in the doorway stood the girl, eyeing him intently with a somber, sullen air. He moved to the door to tell her gently that she had no business there, but she herself spoke before he had time to open his lips.

"I'm not coming in; I know it is not allowed, and I don't want to stay. I've just come to say one last word to you. You have gone on praying though I told you not to, and I've known it. Perhaps you will be satisfied when I tell you that your prayers have been answered and that I'm going away from S. Brioc. You took no notice of me when I told you to stop your prayers: now I tell you that you had better go on praying, because it's owing to you that I'm taking this step and you will be responsible for whatever happens. I have given up all that has made me happy on earth, and you must obtain me the happiness of heaven—for remember, you are responsible for everything. One last word! You'll probably hear one day of Josephine Wheeler—that is, if you haven't heard of her already. So you may as well know, if it is news to you, that Josephine Wheeler is my name."

She gave him one more intent look, turned on her heel and walked out of the Church looking sullen and defiant to the last.

Brother Petroc turned back to the Cope and mechanically settled a fold.

What a curious, uncomfortable place was this twentieth-century England, and what a number of unpleasant, unwholesome people it contained! The woman's words made him shiver in spite of himself: they had sounded almost like a curse. He felt old and chilled and depressed. And he had to face recreation hour with this indefinable weight on him.

Anyhow, responsible or not, he would go on praying for her, but he would not think too much of her as he prayed.

Chapter Thirteen

Petroc was seated at recreation with his Brethren in the Common Room when Dom Maurus came in. The Brother was never very talkative; he made an interested listener, but there was such a gap in time, between the lives of the others and his own, that he felt he had not much to say which would entertain them. In this he was very wrong; the Brethren liked to hear what he had to tell for it was always clear, to the point and well worth listening to; but they respected his reserve and never forced him to talk more than he chose.

Today however he was even quieter than usual. The encounter in the Church had left him disheartened and uneasy. His common sense told him that earnest, heartfelt prayer never under any circumstances wrought harm, but he lived at all times under a great strain, the past fortnight had been wearing to mind and nerves and he felt rather like a sailor trying to steer by the stars on an overclouded night; it required an even greater effort of will than usual to subdue the ever-present sense of bewilderment.

Maurus, the first greetings over, dropped into a vacant chair beside Petroc and glanced at him. He had not seen the younger man since the afternoon when they had gone into the town together, and now he saw on Petroc's face the same half-stunned look of patient endurance he had noticed then. Maurus felt a movement of impatience. What a hopeless, helpless creature he looked! Why ever did he not try to pull himself together?

He turned back to the circle and began to answer greetings. His community rather enjoyed Maurus. They knew him to be an excellent and capable religious; but he was so bland, so bustling, so full of the almost sacred importance of his work that they found it impossible to take him seriously. Yes, he told them, he had had a meal when he got in. It had been a terrible cross-country journey; one had felt tempted at times to get out and push the train on a little; and then at the stations they seemed to be dependent for time-table and changes on the whim of one sleepy porter. However, there he was at last and the final half-hour had been the worst of the journey.

"There has been a very nasty accident," he told them, "just at the junction of our lane and the high road. It was my bad fortune to see the whole thing, whereas if the trains had been anything like up to time I should have missed it. You know Miss Wheeler, the girl who married Symes, the painter, in a Registry Office. I could never understand a decently brought-up Catholic girl getting entangled with a divorced man as she did. Well! she was walking down the lane with as defiant and determined an air as you please. A motor lorry was coming down the road and she walked, straight and deliberately, right under the wheels. I hurried across and gave her Conditional Absolution, of course, though she must have been killed instantaneously. 'Pon my word when I saw the expression of her face I almost had a scruple at giving her Absolution. The driver of the lorry was in a terrible state, but I told him that I had witnessed the whole thing and that he was not responsible for the accident in any way. He was on his own side and sounded the horn before he came to the turning; she walked straight under the wheels as he went past; and he could not help himself. I waited until the police came and then made my statement. I left them dealing with the body. Eh?"

He interrupted himself for from his side came an almost inaudible murmur:

"What made her do it?"

Maurus looked round and saw Petroc's white strained face turned to him. Now the Guest Master had been travelling since early morning and he had just received a nasty shock, both in witnessing the accident and knowing the life and character of the victim. Really this high tragedy air in the poor fool at his side might do for an Elizabethan melodrama, but it was a bit too much of a good thing in ordinary twentieth-century life. Dom Maurus' temper suddenly got the better of him.

"What a question to ask! You know as much about it as anybody," he snapped, and turning his back, gave his full attention to the volleys of questions which were coming from the other monks.

Petroc sat quite still for a few moments, conscious of nothing but an overwhelming desire to get out of the room without attracting notice. It was the first sharp word he had ever received from any of his new Brethren, and it cut like a knife. Moreover he had never heard the idiom before so did not understand its implication. In its literal sense it fitted in so well with the words spoken to him in the Sacristy that he thought Maurus must possess some knowledge of the events leading up to the accident. And coupling these words with his own experience, he felt like a murderer.

The noise in the room deafened him. Silence was absolutely necessary, that he might attain a definite idea of the part he had played in the tragedy. In this babel of question and answer thought was impossible, when he must come to some conclusion as to how far he was partner in the woman's sin. His present need then was for solitude.

So he drove back the question of his own guilt until he should be alone, and devoted all his energies to the task of getting out of the room. Very quietly he rose, crossed to a table on which lay some books, looked at one or two, picked up one and walked with it to the door. No one noticed him going out and he reached his cell alone.

For a while he was totally oblivious of any mental trouble; for the first time in his life he realized the truth of what the Subprior was always telling him, that he had the heart of an old man, which would not stand too big a strain. He sat for a few moments on the window-seat in the air, fighting faintness and nausea. Then finding it unbearable, he crossed to his cupboard. He had always laughed at the Subprior for insisting on his keeping a flask of brandy there; now he was glad of it. He poured out a small quantity, added water, carried it over to his bed, drank it and lay perfectly still, hoping that the deadly sickness would pass. For about an hour he lay, not daring to move hand or foot. Then very cautiously he turned over and sat up. He still felt queer and dizzy, but the sickness had passed, so he got up and moved slowly over to the open window.

As the bodily trouble abated, the mental trouble asserted itself. Was his whole spiritual position so wrong that his very prayers forced people from one sin to a worse one? He had tried to learn modern views, he had tried to live in the present, he had done all he could as far as his light showed him. For weeks now God had been absent from him. Was it because he was so evil as to force his creator to abandon him?

His Master's absence was hard to bear and his inability to realize God's indwelling in his soul. But abandonment meant that God had turned away from a soul that had rejected grace after grace. What had he done to deserve such punishment? He knew that it followed repeated acts of deliberate infidelity; but how he had been guilty he did not know. The very exercise of his will in turning to God seemed an impossibility. And he could not repent of a crime of which he was ignorant—culpably ignorant he knew—but ignorant nevertheless.

Then before his imagination, the picture of the woman lying dead, with a terrible look of defiance on her face, stood clear and vivid; the only living thing in the gloom. He had killed her, pursuing her with the evil prayers of a bad man. She had called him responsible for whatever might happen, and Dom Maurus had said that he knew all about it.

There was a tap, and the Infirmarian opened the door and looked in:

"Aren't you coming down to supper and Compline, Brother Petroc," he asked. Then looking more closely, he added: "Whatever is the matter? You are ill."

Brother Petroc raised a perfectly colorless face and tried to smile.

"Father Subprior always told me my heart was not strong, but I never really believed him until this afternoon. I am better now, but I do not think I can go downstairs again tonight. Will you excuse me to Father Prior, please?"

"You ought to be lying flat, Brother, or at any rate leaning back. I will bring you an easier chair than the one you have got and fetch you some supper."

"A drink only, please, Brother! I still feel too sick to eat."

The Infirmarian hurried away returning presently with a bowl of soul and orders from the Prior to Petroc to rest himself and take life quietly. Petroc submitted gratefully and patiently to the attentions of the Brother; but he was relieved to find himself alone at last, with a small bell at his side and orders to ring it if he felt ill again.

The night passed slowly. Petroc could never after give an account of it even to himself. For hours he fought despair, and a frantic sense of rebellion at his life thus prolonged out of due time, when he might even then be in eternal bliss with his own Brethren. Twice he moved away from the window and sat on the far side of the room, terrified by the overwhelming temptation to throw himself out. A fearful sense of guilt, a passion of loneliness and homesickness, the notion that he was abandoned by God to a reprobate sense and an overwhelming desire to end his pain, fought within him all night. Added to this, imagination had been stirred by the events of the day and escaped from the iron control of his will. He remembered the Subprior's remark about annihilation of distance and pictured the speed and crushing power of trains, motor cars, aeroplane and wireless with an almost frenzied terror; faces too looked at him, twentieth-century faces strained by the speed with which life rushed on, brooding with incessant in-turning on their own souls. He knew himself to be poised solitary in an unknown, incomprehensible world and he felt he would go mad. Yet Petroc stood aloof and watched the combat, firm only in his will to serve God Who asked so much of him.

In the morning he went down to Mass as usual, but for the first time abstained from Holy Communion. How could he ask the God of all Purity to enter the soul of one responsible for the self-murder of another?

After Mass he sought the Novice Master and asked him to hear his Confession. He returned to the Choir afterwards, bent and frail, but steady again, with the air of one who was shouldering a heavy burden in all patience.

The Infirmarian came to his cell after breakfast to see how he did and was horrified at the change wrought in one night. Yesterday morning Petroc had been a little strained and tired-looking, but bright and alert with an almost boyish air. Today he was a feeble old man, bent and going gray. The perplexed Brother kept him upstairs and dosed him with tonics, but his youth seemed gone forever. And on Monday there was the Subprior to be faced.

Chapter Fourteen

The Subprior came home a day earlier than the Abbot.

When he had paid a visit to the Blessed Sacrament, presented himself to the Prior and had a meal, he went upstairs in search of Brother Petroc. He opened the cell door quietly and looked in. Seated on the window-seat was an oldish man, grey-haired and rather bent. But there was no Petroc. The Subprior stepped across the room to investigate matters and discover the identity of the stranger by the window. At the sound of the footstep the grey head moved and the figure turned in the direction of the door. The face was certainly Petroc's, but it was his face such as it used to look months ago, before the Subprior had roused him; quiet and expressionless. It seemed however to have grown suddenly older, and the horrified Subprior perceived, as he came near, that the brown eyes were full of patient pain.

"Good heavens! Man, whatever have they been doing to you? You are ill," he cried.

"I do not think I am ill. But I am growing an old man, Father, a very old man, that is all....And—my head, somehow, does not seem as clear as it used to be. But I am very glad you have come back."

The Subprior gave him one keen look, then sitting down beside him began to talk as he was wont to do. He told of the long white stretch of sand at Seaham with its background of sand hills. He spoke of the smooth sea, which was hardly ever roughened in storm; and of the cockle-gatherers, who wander over the foreshore at low tide. It was not like their own north Cornish coast, and he was glad to be at home again; but it had been very pleasant and quiet there and he felt much rested. And Brother Petroc listened and smiled a little and said a few words once or twice. But when after half an hour the Subprior rose to go, he left with the baffled sensation of one standing outside a locked door with a bunch of keys not one of which will fit the lock.

When he had fairly closed the door of Petroc's cell, the Subprior proceeded to let the storm of his wrath sweep through the house. He found his own subordinate first.

"What has happened to Brother Petroc while I have been away?" he demanded. "He looks shockingly ill and has grown into an old man."

The Brother knew of nothing which could account for the change; he had done his best for Brother Petroc. He had certainly noticed failure in health and strength. He had a heart attack one afternoon which seemed to leave him an old man.

"Perhaps he was fretting for you, Father; he thinks a mighty lot of you."

"Nonsense; Brother Petroc is not one to fret himself ill because I was away; he's far too much sense. Besides he does not care one scrap, in that way, for any living being. How could he?"

The Brother stared; then repeated his assurances of utter ignorance of anything that could have caused Petroc's failing health.

As there was nothing more to be discovered in that direction, the Subprior made his way to the Prior's room.

"What have they been doing to Petroc, Father Prior, while I've been away?" he asked. "He looks desperately ill and terrified half out of his wits."

The Prior had noticed the sudden failure of Petroc's health but of course knew nothing to account for it, so he raised his eyebrows.

"I am quite unaware of anything which has happened to Brother Petroc during your absence," he answered. "He has lived his usual life and been left, as far as I know, in absolute peace. In fact we have seen very little of him. You must surely be prepared for ups and downs in a case like his. Perhaps he was fretting for you or the Abbot. You are both a little inclined to spoil him, you know."

The Subprior shut his lips tight for a second or two, and when he spoke it was with an obvious effort for self-control.

"I can assure you, Father, that Petroc is incapable of fretting either for the Abbot or for me. He is absolutely detached; even from a human point of view, it is almost an inevitable result of his circumstances. And as for any question of spoiling, it is simply God's Mercy and his own magnificent strength of will which has saved him from madness. The least we can do is to ease his lot as far as we are able. None of you seem to realize the constant heavy strain under which he lives, allowing his memory as little freedom as possible in sheer self-defense. No! Something definite has happened to him while I have been away, and I intend to find out."

He left the room and went upstairs to the Novices' quarters.

"May I have a word with the Novices about Brother Petroc, Father?" he asked.

"Certainly," said the Novice Master, and took him to the Library where the Novices were studying.

"Look here, young men. Which of you has been upsetting Brother Petroc?" he demanded.

The Novices were horrified. Not one of them would dream of doing anything to upset Brother Petroc. Brother Petroc was splendid; he had more brains in his little finger than the sum-total of their wits put together. It would be a piece of unpardonable impertinence to take liberties with a man like him. They knew he was ill; he had suddenly changed about two or three days before, but they had absolutely no idea what had upset him. They had talked it over among themselves and had done all they could think of to interest him and take his mind off whatever was worrying him. They were afraid their efforts had not been of much use; he had been as friendly as possible all the time, but he hardly seemed to follow what they were talking about. The Subprior apologized for his suspicions and left them, baffled.

Next morning the Abbot returned and in the evening the Subprior went to his room.

"Something has gone seriously wrong with Brother Petroc," he said. "When I came back yesterday I found him suddenly grown into a broken-down old man. He will hardly speak and seems to shrink into himself when anyone talks to him. He is badly frightened and in some sort of mental trouble. I have made enquiries all round the house, but can discover no reason for this sudden change. Will you come upstairs and see him for yourself?"

"Certainly. I will come up at once. But don't you think this sudden change may be accounted for by the peculiar circumstances of his life? After all, you yourself have always found the heart very weak, and have owned that you did not know what to expect next."

"We might certainly expect him to grow old quicker than other men; a sudden collapse would also be quite understandable; but no merely physical cause would account for the condition in which I found him yesterday. He is obviously suffering from a shock which has in some way affected his spiritual life, and it is this which is reacting on the body. But come up and see for yourself."

They went to Petroc's cell together and found him at work on some printing for the Librarian. Petroc's Gothic print and illuminated capitals were delightful. He smiled as the Abbot entered and, crossing the room, knelt for his blessing. The Abbot gave him one keen glance and then walked over to the table.

"This is a very beautiful piece of work, Brother," he said, bending over the vellum on the table.

"I learnt print and illuminating for many years, Father Abbot; but neither your paint nor your parchment is as good as what we used to use."

The Abbot continued to discuss the question of illumination for a moment or two, then gradually introduced the question of Petroc's failing health. Very gently and with great tact he tried to get to the bottom of the trouble, but he could learn nothing. Petroc owned that his head often felt confused nowadays. It was a strange world and he was a very old man. He had lost God somehow, and though he knew that He was really present, he could not find a way to reach Him. Petroc was too old a fool to learn new ways in the spiritual life and he had forgotten the old. The Abbot turned to say a few words of comfort suggesting that God was, most likely, all the nearer because of the darkness. But Petroc seemed to shrink into himself as soon as he began to speak, and it seemed the more merciful course to leave him alone.

"Something has gone seriously wrong," he owned to the Subprior when they got outside the cell, "but it is an adjustment which is too delicate for us to handle. We must simply take care of his body and pray for his soul. After all Petroc is obviously very close to God, Who will deal with him as he sees best."

Chapter Fifteen

On the outskirts of the town of S. Brioc lived a Catholic artist, who kept a small sailing-boat for use in fine weather. This man was on very friendly terms with the monks and had helped them to decorate the extension of their Church. A very beautiful painted reredos above one of the side Altars had been his work. While he had been painting he had seen quite a lot of the Novices, for one or the other of them had held ladders and done other small services for him. He took a kindly interest in the lads, and in order to give them an extra opportunity for change and fresh air, offered his boat for their use each fine Thursday afternoon in the season. He used to send his boatman with it to the cove belonging to the Monastery, so that there was no need for the Novices to go into the town.

A week or two after their interview with the Subprior the afternoon for their weekly sail came round. The previous afternoon they went in a body to the Novice Master's room to make a petition. Brother Petroc was ill, or in trouble. They had been aware of that fact before the Subprior had mentioned it to them. But if the latter were really as anxious as he had seemed to be, there must be something seriously amiss. Did the Novice Master think they would be allowed to take Brother Petroc out with them next afternoon? It was Ascension Day, so surely that would be a good excuse for the invitation. They would take the greatest care of him and they were sure the change would do him good.

The Novice Master carried their request to the Abbot, who referred him to the Subprior. The latter considered the matter for a moment and then said:

"Even if the change does Brother Petroc no good, I do not see that it can possibly do him any harm. He is brighter with the Novices than with anyone else, and they are good lads. Please tell them that if I trust Petroc to them they must be very careful."

The Novices were delighted and on talking matters over decided on an additional precaution, about which they did not consider it necessary to refer to their Superior.

Brother Petroc was informed of the Novices' request and that it had been acceded to, and was told to meet them at the garden gate at 2.30 prompt. Punctual to the minute, he came slowly down the stairs. At the bottom he was turning into the Church Cloister on his way to the garden, when he ran straight into Dom Maurus.

Maurus was all smiles. He had heard that the Brother was not well, and he himself had been very busy, but he had not relinquished his intention of forwarding the unfortunate monk's interests. So he stepped towards him.

"I am glad to see that you are better, Brother," he said. "Please do not think I have forgotten you. I have been very busy lately, but I hope in a few days we may have an opportunity—"

He ceased abruptly, for Petroc had gone dead white and was leaning back against the wall with an expression in which self-control fought with an almost unsurmountable repulsion. Maurus stared for a second and then began to redden, for he saw that something was very wrong and that he was somehow connected with it. But before he could gather breath to pursue the matter further, Petroc had mastered himself.

"You are very kind, Father," he answered in low, rather shaken tones. "I am an old man and have been somewhat ailing lately. But perhaps when my strength comes back a little—"

He passed on, leaving Dom Maurus somehow conscience-smitten, he did not quite know why.

The Novices were waiting by the garden gate. Their greeting was warm and they made no comment on the color of Petroc's face and the slight trembling in his hands. They conveyed him very slowly down the hill to the little private jetty of the Monastery, where a small, safe cutter was waiting in the yachtsman's charge. They got on board and helped Petroc over the side; then Brother Gregory turned to the man:

"We shall be able to manage nicely by ourselves, thank you. Will you be back for the boat in about three hours' time?"

The man looked surprised and hesitated. But since he was aware that the Novices understood something of managing a boat, he knew of no valid objection. So he leaped ashore and shoved off the boat.

The Novices settled Petroc comfortably in the stern and set off with the wind to skirt the coast westward. Their passenger did not at first seem to pay much heed to anything or anybody. But presently his drawn face began to relax and he spoke a little to Brother Leo at the tiller, asking a few questions relative to the steering of the boat, and saying that he had often sailed a boat, which was however much more clumsy than their present craft, up and down that coast. Brother Leo made a ready response to all that he said, but otherwise they left him sitting quiet.

They spun merrily along the coast for about an hour; then Brother Pius suggested a return.

"We have to go home against the wind," he said.

They turned the boat, and not until then did they realize how strong the breeze was which had carried them west, and how difficult it would be to tack back. However Brother Leo started to make the best of his job. He found it very hard work to keep the mainsail full of wind and to change tack was more difficult than anything he had tried before. He dared not go too close to the rocky coast where the wind was not so strong, and farther out the breeze was more than these very inexperienced sailors liked. However for about half an hour they persevered. Then Brother Gregory touched Brother Leo's arm and pointed to the coast. They were in precisely the same spot as they had been when they turned.

"That's cheerful," said Brother Leo; "it does not look as if we are going to get home at this rate unless the wind shifts. I wonder what we can do?"

"What is the trouble?" asked Brother Pius, making his way to the two at the tiller.

"A mere detail. We have been sailing home for half an hour now and we are precisely in the same spot as we were when we started."

The three looked rather blankly at each other. At this rate they would never be home in time. They would get into trouble for being out beyond the appointed hour, they knew, but what was much more serious, they would not get back until after dark; and to be on the water then would be a positive danger, as they had no compass. Besides they had promised so faithfully to take care of their passenger. As they were consulting together with anxious faces, a hand was laid very gently on Brother Leo's arm.

"Will you allow me, please?" said Petroc, and took the tiller.

The Novices turned and watched wide-eyed. They had never seen a boat handled as the new helmsman handled it. The tacking was so skilful that they seemed to be sailing almost in the eye of the wind. Brother Petroc sat very quietly with an eye on the mainsail and an occasional glance at the coast line. Sometimes he seemed to steer the boat almost ashore, following some channel well known to him; then without apparent reason he would swing out to sea, avoiding some hidden shoal. He turned the boat at last into their own little inlet; but the Novices were so spell-bound that he had to repeat twice the smile and courteous little gesture with which he invited Brother Leo to take the tiller and steer for the landing stage. The boatman was in waiting, they were not more than half an hour beyond time, and the Novices, breathing freely again, bombarded Petroc with eager questions as to how he had managed the task. Petroc smiled a little and answered briefly that he knew the coast well and had often taken a boat out, both as a little lad and later as a Novice.

As they reached the garden door he turned to thank them, adding gently, "If I have been of any service to you, Brothers, pray to God's Mother for me," and went in.

That evening on returning from the tribune to his cell, he went according to his custom to kneel before the statue of Our Lady which stood at the angle of his passage. He looked up at the Blessed Mother's face and said softly:

"Mother of God and my Mother! I have lost your Son for nearly six weeks now; find Him for me again I pray. Or if you will not listen to the prayer of so unworthy a son, hearken at least those of your Novices who make interces me."

As he knelt with upturned face, deep in his soul he heard a voice: Why seek you Him Who is already within you? Hold fast to Him by Faith and Hope and cleave to Him by Charity, then what ever may happen you will always be very safe.

Next morning he did not come down to the Choir, and as soon as Mass was over the anxious Subprior hastened upstairs to find the cause of his absence. He knocked at the cell door and getting no answer went in. There snug in bed lay Brother Petroc fast asleep. One hand rested like a child's under his cheek, the other was twisted in his Rosary. Very quietly the Subprior crept out, and went to post fierce notices on the stairs and in the corridor, demanding absolute silence in that part of the house.

It was afternoon before his patient woke, and with his old bright smile took the dinner the Subprior had brought him. His nurse laughed at him and teased him gently, hiding his anxiety and relief under a joking manner. But he could elicit nothing from Petroc beyond the smiling statement that his good Mother would not leave her child too long alone in the dark. He never gave more details; probably he could not.

Henceforward he was quiet but serene, with a look of almost unearthly peace on his face. He was found in his wonted place in Choir and Refectory; otherwise the Community saw very little of him.

Whitsun came and went and the beautiful feast of Corpus Christi; Brother Petroc watched the Procession in the grounds from his cell window, but the Subprior feared to let him walk with the rest.

On June 20th the Abbot and his Council met to discuss the question of Petroc's ordination. Very reluctantly it was decided that it would be unwise to risk any further disturbance by beginning even the minimum of study necessary for the priesthood. Brother Petroc must live and die a simple Choir Brother.

The Abbot promised the Subprior that he himself would break the news to the old man. The

Subprior owned that it would be an impossibility to him, and he dreaded the effect of the news however carefully it was broken.

However the Brother had to be told, so the Abbot went out to him in the Cloister garth the next afternoon and told him as gently as he could of the decision of the Council.

Brother Petroc paused for a moment, half turned from the Abbot and bending the face of a tall sunflower towards him, looked at it intently. Then he turned back to the Abbot.

"God's Will is always beautiful, Father Abbot," said Brother Petroc with a tranquil smile.

The Abbot reassured the Subprior at once, telling him that his patient had taken the news quite calmly and had continued his walk afterwards with no trouble whatever visible on his face. The Subprior, remembering the look with which Petroc had greeted his assurance that he was to begin his studies almost immediately, was frankly puzzled. However resigned to God's will the old man might be, it was surely impossible for him not to feel great disappointment.

He did not see Petroc however until late in the afternoon and then they met in the Library. He had hurried in to look up a reference and ran straight into the Brother bringing out a book from which he wanted to copy a border for the Altar cards he was illuminating. The Subprior pulled up short on seeing whom he had run into, and apologized. Petroc smiled and then told him quite quietly that all hope of the priesthood was now at an end.

"I'm sorry," said the Subprior, and then stopped. It was so difficult to find words adequate to the occasion.

"It is God's beautiful Will," answered Petroc, repeating the words he had used to the Abbot.

The Subprior looked at him keenly. His face was perfectly serene and there seemed no suppressed disappointment hidden behind it.

"I wish I could guess what is going on at the back of that calm exterior," he muttered to himself, completely baffled.

Petroc caught the words and smiled a little.

"You foolish, foolish people of this later time," he answered. "Why must you always be searching into the depth of your own heart and those of others? Why must you always seek to express the incorporeal in terms of matter? Does the search bring aught but anxiety and dissatisfaction?"

"I am sorry, Brother," said the Subprior; "truly it is my affection for you and not curiosity which makes me want to understand. I would like, if I could, to help you."

Petroc smiled again.

"Consider, Father," he said. "You are the best friend I have here on this earth and it is you who have given me all I have. But between the rest of living men and myself four hundred years hang like an impenetrable curtain. Your mode of life, your thoughts and your motives are beyond my ken, neither can you understand me. I have endeavored to bridge this gulf; I have learnt what I might concerning the development of the race and its changed way of living, its wonderful inventions and the way it adapts itself to its changed circumstances. But my mind has not the changed outlook that four hundred years have given yours, and so I found the gulf could not in that way be bridged.

"Then I saw that your Religious life, here in this Monastery, in externals much resembled mine, so I hoped that in this way I might reach you and live in the present as Father Abbot bade me. But I learnt that there were abroad other far different forms of living the Religious life, and that even here your minds, so different from mine own, approached our common duties in another spirit. Nearest to me in thought came Brother Leo, but even he was not as I.

"I tried thus in the only two ways that I knew to bridge the gulf, but I found it impassable. Moreover the struggle I made was rendering me difficult to live with and very wearisome to myself.

"Lastly after much tribulation it seemed to me that our only place of meeting was in God. So I turned from this world as from a dream impossible to understand and ceased to strive to bridge the gulf between it and me. But in God and in His beautiful Will, my Father, I have found you and my Brothers.

"There is our common meeting-ground; for we all watch in prayer to learn more about Him, and in our life we strive to come closer to Him. We use the same means; namely the Psalms of David, the Sacrifice of the Mass and a Common life. And so, since I have found you all, I am no longer solitary and unlike the rest, and in this I am very happy. But I fear to lose you again, so I cling with all my strength to God's beautiful Will, and I turned my eyes away from the differences which four hundred years have made. Now if you really love me, Father, as I truly believe you do, you also will turn away from all those things which make me so unlike you and which you can never understand, but you will meet me in God and His beautiful Will, where no shadow of perplexity can come between us."

"And what of this life passing now, with all the things which must be so strange to you?"

"Shadows, Father, the shadows of a dream. There is only one reality."

The Subprior stood for a second fingering his Rosary. It was somehow difficult to speak. Then he said very quickly and gruffly:

"Very well! I'll come to you if I can."

Then with a quick change of tone, "Now for goodness' sake, help me to verify this quotation from S. Augustine; I don't think I have it quite correct as to words, and I have written an article which must go out by this post."

Apparently Brother Petroc understood the request and tone in which it was made, for he laughed a little as he moved across the room to the shelf which was reserved for S. Augustine's works.

Chapter Sixteen

It was the feast of SS. Peter and Paul and the Bishop had written to say he was coming next day to the Abbey to discuss some business matters with the Abbot. He added that he would very much like to see the monk who had been miraculously preserved from death. The Subprior told Petroc of this part of the letter, and he smiled in some amusement. It was strange what an important part Petroc was beginning to play in the life of the Monastery; for the Novices no longer had the monopoly of affection and admiration for the Brother. In the last few months, Petroc had grown a white-haired, frail old man; and it may have been partly this fact and partly a certain atmosphere of serene happiness which surrounded him, that fostered a general habit in the Community of seeking Petroc when the stress of life grew heavy. When the Prior was worn out with business, he would slip up to the Infirmary cell and after sitting quietly on the window-seat for a few minutes would leave the old man, rested. If a monk were in trouble, difficulty or temptation it had become a regular custom to seek Brother Petroc. He listened readily to all that was told him but said very little himself. When the other had quite finished he would smile and say that God was always near, and His Will was always beautiful; though sometimes there were only Faith, Hope and Charity to hold Him with. It was enough however; for these three were all that was needful and their use depended on God's Grace, which never failed the suppliant, and man's own will, which was always free. But though his words were few and simple his mere presence, bright smile and courteous ways carried with them an extraordinary efficacy. The Abbot, whose opinion of Petroc was very high, encouraged his Community to see much of him, and very readily granted permission to speak to him. There was only one monk who avoided him. After their chance meeting in the cloister, Dom Maurus, conscious of having in some way injured one he sincerely intended to benefit, though still ignorant of the precise nature of his offence, dreaded a repetition of the painful little scene and kept out of his way.

Brother Petroc felt some mild interest in the arrival of my Lord Bishop and his retinue. He did not know very much about such happenings, for the Oath of Supremacy and the Schism which had resulted therefrom had precluded Episcopal visits in the days of his youth. Only once in his memory had the Bishop of Exeter visited S. Brioc's, and that was in 1532, the year that he had come, a small alumnus, to the Monastery. Petroc recollected the bustle of preparation which pervaded the house. The Procurator had been a very busy man for days beforehand. There had been a great slaughter of lambs, calves and a whole litter of little suckling pigs in the farm. Three of the Brethren had spent the preceding day sea-fishing, while two more had taken rods and gone for peel and trout. Then there had been a mighty stir in the kitchen and bakehouse, with Lay Brothers in aprons hurrying here and there.

In the end he had climbed out on the roof—a feat for which he had received well-merited punishment from the Master of the Children—and had watched the cavalcade ride up, the Churchmen on mules and the Gentlemen of the Household following on horseback. He remembered the small page who held the Bishop's stirrup, and the procession of monks standing at the door to greet his Lordship. He could still see the crowded refectory, where he had been one of the boys appointed to wait at the Abbot's table; that was before his escapade on the roof was discovered; for when that came to light he had promptly disappeared from public life. For quite twenty-four hours after that visit he had debated with himself whether or no the frock of a secular priest, with its chance of a bishopric, were preferable to the monk's cowl. In the end he had decided that the opportunity of being a mitred Abbot was a more likely one.

Next year the Oath of Supremacy was administered and the Abbot received private intimation from the Bishop, an old school-fellow of his, that the name of his Monastery, an unimportant place in an unfrequented spot, had been omitted from the list of Religious Houses in the diocese. So the Benedictines had been left in peace, but there were of course no more Episcopal visits. Still, the monks were always looking forward to better times; and the older ones would tell tales of bygone greatness, when the visits of great persons to the Monastery were red-letter days. Now apparently these days had returned and Petroc would once more witness the ceremonial attached to the arrival of a Lord

Bishop and his retinue. He was rather surprised therefore to see so few signs of bustle and commotion. Everything seemed to be going on precisely as usual; and the Procurator even found time to bring Petroc an early bunch of grapes.

When the dinner hour came he glanced round, expecting to find the refectory full of guests; but there was only one tall, thin priest—a bishop's chaplain possibly by his dress—seated at the Abbot's table. Petroc decided that my Lord had not come after all and dismissed the thing from his mind.

After dinner he went, according to orders, to his cell to rest. The Subprior had installed a big chair by the window and bade the old man use it. Petroc was more than a little in awe of that chair.

As he sat Rosary in hand, half asleep, there was a gentle tap and the door opened. Petroc rose to find the Abbot in the doorway with the tall stranger.

"I have brought the Bishop up to see you, Brother," said the Abbot. And Petroc, wholly amazed, dropped on one knee to kiss the ring presented to him. Courtesy forbade any comment then; but afterwards when he thrashed the whole question of retinue out with the Subprior, he showed a touch of his old keenness.

"I have been wanting to see you for some time, Brother," the Bishop began. "I heard your tale, of course, at the time when it happened, from Father Abbot, and I was very much interested in the whole matter. It seems then that Our Lady preserved your life in order that you may receive the priesthood. I hope you will be ordained shortly."

"I am afraid all hope of that is over now, my Lord. I am an old man, and my head has grown too stupid to learn what is necessary," answered Petroc.

"Is this decision your own, Brother?" If not, I think a way can be found to surmount the difficulty. A very small minimum would be required in your case. Can you explain why all hope of ordination is over, as you say?"

"It is God's beautiful Will, not mine," said Petroc tranquilly.

"Still it must be the subject of great grief to you, Brother, and you must feel this frustration of all your hopes a very bitter trial."

"I have not questioned my feelings, my Lord, when I know it is God's Will."

"Did you learn how to say Mass in those faraway years?"

"Oh yes, my Lord, I was within two days of receiving the priesthood."

"And do you still remember how to say it, Brother?"

"Could one ever forget, my Lord? Perhaps one or two details have slipped my memory, but very little."

"Father Abbot," the Bishop half turned and Petroc moved to the window to watch the circling gulls and silver-flecked sea, "if Brother Petroc remembers how to say Mass and if all the circumstances of his case are carefully explained at Rome, I have no doubt but that the Pope would give permission for his ordination at once without further study. I could certainly get permission, if it were necessary, for him to say a Votive Mass of Our Lady. The Vicar-General leaves for Rome on business tomorrow. I shall get back in time to see him tonight and will put him thoroughly *au courant* with the details of this matter, besides giving him a written petition. If you will also give me a petition on your own behalf, I will tell Monsignor Dunn to get in touch immediately with the proper authorities, and to forward the matter as far as he can. I will direct him to cable if he gets a favorable answer, and in this way it ought to be possible to arrange for the ordination privately on August the 15th. What do you think, Brother Petroc"—he raised his voice and Petroc left the window—"of our trying to obtain leave from the Pope to ordain you, without any more study, on the anniversary of that day when you should have been made a priest nearly four hundred years ago?"

Petroc went from red to white and his hands locked tightly. But he held every other expression of emotion in check and answered very quietly:

"I am Father Abbot's subject, my Lord, and my will is in conformity with his wishes."

"And suppose, my son, that Father Abbot says that his will is in full accordance with his Lordship's," said the Abbot.

Petroc's face lighted up. "Then, my Lord, then"—but his eyes had to give the answer his lips could not frame.

The Bishop smiled. "Then we must see what can be done about it. God bless you, Brother," and he turned to the door.

"I wonder if the world has ever known so lonely a soul as that must be?" he said as they came into the corridor.

The Abbot caught his breath. That aspect of the case had never occurred to him before, but now he came to think of it...

Chapter Seventeen

The Abbot kept his own counsel about the petition which had gone to Rome for Brother Petroc's ordination, until the Bishop wired to him that the necessary permission had been obtained and was even now on its way to England. He wrote next day that he would come down and ordain the candidate as quietly as possible on August 15th, but would be obliged if the Abbot could make it convenient to spend a night at the Bishop's house before then, so that they might make arrangements for the ceremony to be as short and easy as possible for Brother Petroc.

That evening in the Common Room the Abbot told the Community what had happened and of the special leave for ordination which had been obtained by the Bishop.

"The whole affair has been rather incomprehensible," he said. "Brother Petroc was gaining strength, both of mind and body, so rapidly that Father Subprior and I decided that it was quite possible for him to prepare as a candidate for ordination. He is already a Deacon, and went through his studies for the priesthood in the first stages of his life; besides the Bishop of course knew all about him, so that everything would have been quite simple. We made up our minds last Easter that as soon as Father Subprior and I came home after the month we had to spend away, his course of study should begin. Father Subprior would probably have been his tutor, as he understands him so thoroughly, and it is only fair to make things as easy as possible for a man in his difficult position. We left a vigorous young man, and came back at the end of a month to find a broken-down, old one, utterly unfit to follow the most carefully planned course of study. We cannot imagine what can have happened to him during our absence. He either cannot or will not say anything. At first I was inclined to think it the natural consequence of his condition and circumstances. Father Subprior however was certain he had had some severe kind of shock, and he soon convinced me. This shock, whatever it was, reacted in some way on his spiritual life, which in its turn affected his physical condition.

"The trouble, whatever it was, appeared to be lifted as suddenly as it had come. Here again we know very little definitely, except that Our Lady was connected somehow with his restored peace of mind. He is able to speak very little about himself. But nothing, however, can restore him to his former physical condition; for though this decay of bodily powers was hastened by the shock he had had, his heart was always weak and he is now to all intents and purposes a very old man.

"However, the Bishop was extraordinarily impressed by him, and considered that we should be doing not only him but the Church in general an injustice by neglecting to apply for a dispensation for him to be ordained. Now that it has been granted, the only thing left for us to do is to make sure that he remembers every detail in the celebration of Mass."

The Community were deeply interested in what they had just been told and the remainder of the recreation passed quickly in discussion and comment. But Dom Maurus sat silent, turning over the pages of a Review and taking no apparent interest in the talk around him. When the Abbot rose to go, he followed and asked permission to speak to him in his room; for at last the Guest Master realized to the full what he had done, and being a straightforward man he took his tale at once to the Superior.

"I am sorry to say, Father, that I have just realized that I am the probable cause of Brother Petroc's broken health."

"Nonsense!" said the Abbot. "How can that possibly be when you never come in contact with him?"

"He spent an afternoon out with me while you were away, Father; I took him for a walk and did some visiting on the way."

"I suppose you had Father Prior's permission to take Brother Petroc out?"

"Yes, Father, certainly. But I do not think Father Prior was paying much attention when he gave the permission. He was very busy with his post when I went in and said Yes as though he hardly realized what I was asking."

"This permission was not taken as an easy way of getting something you wanted, and did not think I should allow, if I were at home, I am sure?"

"Oh no! Father. I had never noticed Brother Petroc much while you and Father Subprior were at home. Your remarks about his beginning to study as soon as you returned roused my interest in him, and I came to the conclusion that he was not getting a fair chance and that I might help. If you had been at home I should have come to you, stated my views and asked your permission to take Brother Petroc out. I went into no details with Father Prior simply because I did not think he was interested in the Brother."

"Where did you take him, please?"

"We went into the town to the Convent of the Daughters of Fortitude, then on to Miss Jackson's, and Captain Branksome's. We came home over the cliffs."

"You took Brother Petroc down into the congested traffic of that cramped little town? You ought to be on your knees thanking God he did not go mad there and then. Father Subprior and I have never dared allow him to face any noise or bustle; his whole nervous system is far too delicate to risk shocks of any kind. I imagine, since you are supposed to possess at least an average amount of common sense, that you had some motive in all this madness. Will you explain please?"

"When you spoke of Brother Petroc's preparing for the priesthood I came to the conclusion that you and Father Subprior were not giving him a fair chance; keeping him, as I thought, so carefully apart from any contact with life outside. I did not see how he could possibly prepare for the priesthood without some knowledge of the world and modern thought. So I thought a visit to the town might give him ideas on a very small scale. Then I took him to the Convent and asked Reverend Mother to tell him of their life and spiritual exercises. Next we went to Miss Jackson's to show him the danger of an uncontrolled seeking after mysticism. Then, as we came home, I explained things to him. He seemed very quiet and uninterested but I did not realize until I met him some days later that I had somehow frightened him. And it was only tonight that I discovered what I had done."

"You took a man who had no conception of the meaning of the Reformation, a man whose ideas are those of the Ages of Faith, and whose piety is as simple as that of a child; you took this man, without any preliminary explanation, without attempting to find out whether he would be able to understand anything he was going to hear, and introduced him to a form of spirituality of whose very existence he had no previous idea, and then showed this unfortunate man, a mystic who is totally unaware of the fact, a woman like Miss Jackson? If you had not told me yourself, I should not have believed such criminal foolishness possible. It is fortunate that only the poor body has been broken and not the mind and soul as well. Superiors, Father, though they be fools, have the Grace of Office, which enlightens them as to the wisest treatment for those in their charge. Whereas clever men simply act like fools when they prefer their own knowledge to this grace-given wisdom. I hardly think I need say anymore. The knowledge of what you have actually done, and still more of what you might have done, will be sufficiently painful without any additional words of mine."

Dom Maurus prostrated. Then, after a moment's pause said very humbly:

"It is my obvious duty to try and make some reparation to Brother Petroc. But I do not see what I can do. The very sight of me must be painful to him. So I suppose the only reparation possible to me is to keep as far as I can from him."

The Abbot picked up a paper-knife and began to trace patterns on the blotting-paper with its tip. Then he said in an impersonal and business-like tone:

"Brother Petroc must study the Missal a little and have a few lessons in the rubrics and ceremonies of the Mass. You, Father Maurus, will teach him; and the Holy Spirit will show you the rest. Please begin tomorrow afternoon."

Dom Maurus gasped. It is the custom to acknowledge the injunction of an Abbot by an inclination of the head, and perhaps it was as well for the monk that no more was expected of him.

"One last thing, Father Maurus, you are not to repeat what you have told me this afternoon to anyone." Then as Dom Maurus appeared to hesitate, "I am not trying to spare you in any way; I am only thinking of Brother Petroc, and your acknowledgment will be certain to raise a storm. Father Subprior for one will be furious, and that storm will be equally certain to react somehow on Brother Petroc. He has already suffered more than enough through contact with us; we must spare him everything we can."

Dom Maurus left the room and the Abbot sat still, toying with the paper-knife. He was more disturbed by what he had just heard than he had let the other know; for to allow a second person to be broken over the affair would not help Petroc in any way. The Abbot realized, as no one except the Subprior could have done, what that afternoon must have cost Petroc. The journey through the town was bad enough, but the calls they had paid were far worse. If he had been merely introduced to Revered Mother all would have been well; he would have appreciated her very real holiness, and the way by which she had attained it would have troubled him not at all. For Petroc was a member of one of the older Orders who discipline the body that the soul may go free, and had never come in contact with that heresy that struck so deeply at Free Will that it became necessary to spare the body in order to discipline the soul. All Religions, nowadays, understand that it is necessary for such discipline to be present in the Church, and its great usefulness for some souls; even if they themselves follow the older way. But to the sixteenth-century monk, who had no such knowledge, the whole matter must have been a painful enigma. The crowning horror of the afternoon, however, must have been the visit to Miss Jackson; unless indeed by then he was so stunned by all he had gone through before as to be mercifully unconscious of the almost pathetic parody of real and beautiful things which was exemplified in that lady. The Abbot almost shuddered himself as he thought of the juxtaposition of Petroc and Miss Jackson. No wonder the strain of that afternoon had broken the unfortunate monk. However, no good was to be gained by contemplating the irrevocable; and in the event, what ought to have driven Petroc insane had, on the contrary, contributed to a very real growth in sanctity. So the Abbot, with a sigh, turned to his letters.

Next afternoon Dom Maurus armed himself with a large Missal and made his way to Brother Petroc's cell. He paused for a moment before knocking, in order to gather his energies. He had a very trying ordeal before him and so he feared had Petroc; but his scholar would only find it endurable if Maurus were very matter-of-fact and impersonal. So he entered quietly and said:

"I hope this is not an inconvenient time for you, Brother, for Father Abbot has given me the honor of preparing you to say Mass, and I think we had better begin as soon as possible. Please do not get up,"

Brother Petroc went white, and his hands sought the arms of his chair, but he answered quite calmly:

"I am an old man, Father, a very stupid old man, I fear; but if you will have patience with me, I will do my best."

"Stay just as you are in your chair, Brother; see, we can manage nicely, this way." And, drawing a table up, Maurus placed the open Missal on it. First he said a few words about the different places which were indicated by the bookmarks, then he invited Petroc to begin, saying that he would take the server's part. But it would not do. Petroc made pitiful and most heroic efforts to fulfill the part assigned to him, but he trembled all over and stammered over the simplest words while of the ceremonies he seemed to have no recollection at all.

The situation was rapidly becoming unbearable, and yet Maurus could think of no way to relieve it. It was obviously out of the question for him to say anything, for that would only crystallize the difficulty and make matters worse. Yet something must be done quickly. As the old man at his side stumbled and stammered on, his teacher prayed desperately to the Holy Ghost and Our Lady. Then suddenly as he prayed, inspiration came to him.

Very quietly he lifted the table to one side; then, before Petroc realized in the very least what he was going to do, he knelt and kissed the old man's feet.

There was a gasp of horror, and for a second Petroc drew back. Then suddenly enlightenment came to him likewise, and in a flash he understood what the gesture meant. Leaning quickly forward, he placed both hands on the kneeling man's shoulders and gave him the Kiss of Peace.

The situation had been so tense and its lightening so dramatic that the self-contained Dom Maurus forgot to feel embarrassed at his unusual demonstration.

After that the lessons proceeded at a great pace, and Brother Petroc was soon ready for Friday August 15th.

Chapter Eighteen

The Abbot walked slowly along the passage to Brother Petroc's cell, fingering the note he carried in his hand. About half-way down the corridor, he halted at an open window and stood, still fingering the note and thinking deeply. He had just come from a rather poignant interview with a visitor who had asked him to communicate something to Brother Petroc, and he hardly knew how to do it. At last he squared his shoulders with the air of a man who saw his way clear and tapped at Petroc's door.

The old man rose at his Superior's entrance, but the Abbot pushed him gently back into his chair and seated himself on the window-seat.

"Do you remember a day last February, Brother, when you took me to see the first daffodils and told me about a mad woman who had spoken to you?"

Brother Petroc changed color and seemed to shrink into himself for a moment. Then he nodded.

"That same woman was killed, just at the bottom of our lane, by a lorry a few weeks ago. She had gone through the ceremony of marriage with a man who already had a wife, and had lived with him for some weeks. The day she was killed, her mother received a letter from her which I am going to read to you:

"MOTHER DEAREST,

"You may own me as your daughter again because I'm leaving Henry today. A monk of S. Brioc's, with a face that is half a boy's and half an angel's, said he would pray for me, and he has left me no peace day or night since I came here. And so I'm leaving Henry. I'm slipping off without telling him, because he would never let me go without a struggle to keep me and I love him too much to risk it. I can get work at my old school; the headmistress told me she could always find a place for me. I can't stop near S. Brioc, or even come to see you, because I'm afraid to trust myself. I mean to tell the Brother who is responsible for all this to go on praying for me—that is, if I can see him. Don't write to me until I write again for I'm too utterly miserable to bear even a word of kindness.

JOSIE

"Miss Wheeler, then, must have come down the lane after trying to see you when she met with her accident. The mother, who came to see me this afternoon—she has been too ill to come before—felt it was only fair to you to let you know that, under God, her daughter owes her eternal Salvation to you and your prayers."

"Eternal Salvation! Father Abbot, she herself was the cause of her death, she ran deliberately under the wheels of the lorry."

"No! No! Brother, that was cleared up at the inquest. Miss Wheeler was a very clever, very sensitive woman, who had been well taught, and was determined to conceal her affliction from everyone; but she was stone deaf. She was so preoccupied with her trouble and the struggle she was making to do right that she was totally oblivious of the need of watching and her ears could give her no warning. So the verdict of accidental death was returned and it is most certainly the true one. Ah! where is the brandy?"

For Petroc was lying back in his chair with closed eyes and a deadly white face. The Abbot rummaged round until he found what he wanted. Then as soon as the color came back to the old man's face he was for calling the Subprior, but Petroc begged him so earnestly to stay that he sat down again.

"You can tell me more about this incident, Brother?" he asked.

"Yes, Father Abbot. The afternoon that the woman was killed, she came up the Church and stood in the Sacristy door. I was about to tell her that she was not allowed there, but she said that she was not coming in. She was simply there to tell me that in consequence of my prayers she was going away, and that whatever befell I should be responsible. I knew naught of her history, so I did not realize what she meant, and though the look in her face almost made me shudder, I added a prayer to the Blessed Mother for her straightaway. Then Dom Maurus came home with the tale of the accident, saying that she had walked deliberately under the lorry and I thought of her words and her face. When I asked Dom Maurus what had made her do that deed, he replied that I knew as much as anyone; so I concluded that he really knew more than he had told us, and that part of this additional knowledge was that I had slain a woman by my prayers. Your age is so full of marvels that yet another machine which would enable a man to obtain such knowledge seemed to me not impossible. That night was a hard one, and next day I dared not receive my Lord's Body into so evil a soul. After Mass I asked the Novice Master to shrive me, and he bade me have no fear, for prayers said in faith and earnestness could never bring a soul to harm. He told me likewise that God had withdrawn His Presence as a trial of my love for Him, and not on account of my sins. And he bade me endure in patience and love until God's Mother should tell me where to find her Son."

"Then your illness was not the direct consequence of that mad walk into S. Brioc on which Dom Maurus took you?"

"I was shaken and disturbed, Father Abbot. And for some days the world seemed a strange and difficult place, very different from that in which I had once lived. But Brother Leo comforted my soul, somewhat, for he spoke to me of spiritual things in a tongue I knew, and assured me that the differences between my Brethren and myself lay in accidentals and not in any deep essential. So I made up my mind to trust God and to use the wit He had given me to find my way; and then things grew easier."

"But Dom Maurus was the real cause of your break-down, nevertheless?"

"The words he said, 'You know as much about it as anybody,' came as such an apt confirmation of my sense of guilt that I could bear no more."

"Yet those words were merely an impatient rejoinder, meaning that, as no one knew anything, you were as wise as they."

"Your manner of speech is strange to me, Father Abbot. So often the words you use signify one thing in fact, while in intention they have a far different meaning. However, Dom Maurus is my very good friend and I would not have him distressed by learning of the pain he had once given to an old fool. And likewise, since the poor mad woman is no self-murderer the rest no longer signifieth. So keep the knowledge you have gained this afternoon for yourself alone, my Father. To spread it further would be merely to bring unnecessary distress."

Chapter Nineteen

It was August 17th, just two days after the ordination of Father Petroc.

On August 15th the Bishop had come and conferred the priesthood on him as quietly and briefly as possible; for in fifteen months Petroc had grown from a youth into a frail old man. The Subprior never left his side, and as soon as the ceremony was ended carried him off to bed. The pulse was so feeble and the whole frame so exhausted that they feared death would come then and there. But he rallied again, and it was decided that after a day spent very quietly in his cell he would be fit to say his first Mass on August 17th. Everything was arranged to spare him. As the 17th was a Sunday, the Abbot decided that he was to say Mass in a little chapel in the house in which there was a consecrated Altar, and that he, the Abbot only, was to be present. The Subprior however would hear of no one but himself serving the Mass.

Father Petroc had been very serene and happy all day on the 16th. In the Morning he said his prayers and watched the seagulls; in the afternoon he asked to see the Novices.

They came in high glee and ensconced themselves on the window-seat, on the table and cross-legged on the floor, telling him in their own fashion how pleased they were that he had been ordained at least. They also gave him further details of their boating expedition with him, and how they had decided to leave the boatman behind so that their passenger might be more at ease; and what the Novice Master had said on that head after they had reached home. They had never realized before that day what a remarkable capacity for expressing himself the Father Master possessed!

Brother Petroc, on his side, had talked more than his wont, telling his guests of his own Novitiate days. There were differences in detail of course, but the main outlines were the same; and Benedictine Novices of the sixteenth century were remarkably like their present-day Brethren.

The Subprior, likewise, had done his duty by sending the Brother Infirmarian in with a feast-day tea, so that they might all picnic up there together. Brother Leo swept up the crumbs after with a patent contrivance made of two sheets of paper, so that the gulls also might share in the celebration.

In the evening the Subprior had come in and seated himself on the window-seat opposite the old man's chair. Petroc had smiled across at him and spoken to him likewise of his Novitiate days and the Spiritual Life that was carried on in the house and of the lessons his Master had taught him of forsaking self to find God.

"New or old," he said, "there is really very little difference. God dwells in the centre of a pure heart. Some reach Him and prepare a dwelling for Him by clearing away all obstacles. Others cleave to Him by Faith, Hope and Charity, fixing their gaze on Him and by the very intensity of that gaze, remove, without much conscious reversion to self, all that is contrary to Him. Even as a painter watches his model and a musician his music-sheet, so do these souls watch God, glancing but now and again at the copy they strive to make of Him in their souls. Provided the end, union with God by Charity, is reached, what do the means matter? I was taught to strive after Him by the latter way, and I am too old to learn any other. Besides, so long as I really strive to attain my end, it is foolishness to leave the familiar way for one that is strange, even if in itself it is a better one. Only one thing really matters, and that is the possession of God, which we attain in this life by

Faith, Hope and Charity, though in the Blessed Life beyond Charity alone remains."

When the Subprior rose to go, he said with a smile:

"I am saying an early Mass tomorrow, so that I shall be free to serve yours later."

Petroc looked up.

"'Twould be better to serve it fasting if you can. Or if you would suffer it so, say a later Mass after mine and then it would serve me for thanksgiving."

"Brother Petroc, Brother Petroc," said the Subprior, smiling again, but watching him keenly and somewhat anxiously at the same time, "I am afraid you are growing exacting. What reason should you have for asking me to go fasting, except that you do not like me to break my fast before you break yours"

"May be, may be," said Petroc, and nodded his head once or twice.

"However, since you will have it so, I will say a later Mass and serve yours first. Goodnight, Brother," and the Subprior left the room.

When his nurse called him next morning, he found the old man wonderfully strong, and as alert mentally as he had been in the days before the Subprior had gone to Seaham. He smiled when he was offered the help of the Brother Infirmarian and answered that he was very well indeed and preferred to dress himself.

When he was ready, he went to the tribune for the sick, until the Subprior called him into the improvised sacristy to vest. This he did quickly and deftly and began Mass in a collected and businesslike way which astonished and delighted the Abbot and Subprior. He seemed to have regained his youth.

He said the Words of Consecration over the Host; then after a moment's pause he gathered himself for the Elevation. In the same firm, collected fashion he proceeded to the Consecration of the Wine, elevated the Chalice and set it down quietly. After that he rested both hands on the Altar and his head and body appeared to droop a little. The Subprior was just preparing to go to his help, when he slowly raised himself to his full height.

"*Nunc dimittis...*" cried Brother Petroc, and fell.

He was quite dead when they reached him; so they laid him, vested as he was, at the foot of the Altar steps, while the Subprior finished the Mass.

About the Author

Sister Mary Catherine Anderson, O.P. was born Kathleen Agnes Cicely Anderson on January 21, 1888 in Falmouth, Cornwall, England. Born to an Anglican clergyman, Kathleen converted with her family to the Catholic Church when still a little girl. She was educated by the Stone Dominican Sisters at their convent of St. Marychurch and entered the congregation on May 2, 1908 at St. Dominic's Convent, Stone, receiving the religious name of Sister Mary Catherine. Sister made her profession on November 25, 1909 and afterwards trained as a primary school teacher at the Sacred Heart Training College in St. Charles's Square, London.

By 1936, when Sister was assigned to St. Marychurch, she had begun to write—mainly historical novels of the revolts in Devon and Cornwall. It was during this time that Sister wrote her most popular book, *Brother Petroc's Return*, which received great acclaim in both England and America. Following this came many other titles including two biographies—*Steward of Souls* and *A Treasure of Joy and Gladness*—as well as lives of St. Margaret of Hungary and of St. Hyacinth.

After her retirement she was appointed prioress to the community in Kelvedon, Essex and then assigned to the convent in Brewood where she continued to write. She died at Stone on April 14, 1972 in the 85th year of her life and the 63rd year of religious profession.